# Summerlands

# Jane Nicholls

# DEDICATION

This labour of love is dedicated to my mother who gave me the amazing
gift of the love of language.

# CONTENTS

# ACKNOWLEDGMENTS

With enormous gratitude to my daughter, Nancy, who supported me all the way, and importantly, thanks to the wonderful and inspiring students and English teachers at St Peters School, Bournemouth and The Grange School in Christchurch.

# MIKEY

They've told me to write down my account of what happened that night. They say it might help stop my nightmares.

I just wish I hadn't forgotten my blazer. It was brand new and it cost my mum a lot of money.

I was in bed nearly asleep, going over the day in my head. I always do that when I'm falling asleep.

I was thinking about Simon saying he'd brought his ball so we could have a kickabout in the park on the way home from school. I remembered getting really hot and taking my blazer off. I didn't put it in my rucksack though, I just folded it roughly and threw it under the nearest tree.

It was a good kickabout.  We were playing in pairs. Me and Simon v Henry and William. We played rush goalie. I'd just scored an amazing goal against Will and I was tearing around doing my victory routine which involves two cartwheels and a handspring when Simon suddenly remembered that he had to meet his little sister from after-school gym. He scooped up the ball and ran across the park in a big hurry.

The rest of us just picked up our rucksacks and sloped off chatting about the Tottenham v Arsenal game that was on that night.

I had definitely left it there. I completely woke up. I looked at the digital clock. It said 23.00 - eleven o'clock.  I thought if I sneak out to the park now and fetch it nobody will ever know I forgot it.

Dad was working the night-shift. Mum would definitely be asleep because she has to get up really early for the morning shift at the hospital.

Joseph, my baby bro' shares my bedroom. He's five and just started school. He was so fast asleep, sucking his thumb and clutching his yellow blankie. I knew he wouldn't wake up till morning.

I put on my trackies and a hoodie over my pjs and crept out of the room. I shut it very quiet behind me.

By the front door I got my house-key from the hook and tucked it deep into my pocket. Then I put on my trainers and headed out the door. I had to pull it three times before it shut. It's hard to close a heavy front door without making a noise.

I ran down the cold concrete steps. When I got to the fire- exit door a loud snore made me jump. I looked under the stairwell to see Ernest, our neighbourhood rough-sleeper, fast asleep under a pile of smelly duvets, behind a row of baby buggies.

I pushed down the bar on the door and I was out. I let the door back softly so that I could get in again when I got back.

There was no-one in sight as I ran across the grass and concrete behind the flats. It was very quiet. I could hear only the hum of faraway traffic on the main road.

I only had to run up one street. After that there are two linked back alleyways to the park. Here and there I woke up dogs and they started barking. I triggered those security lights as I ran past. It seemed much farther than in the daytime.

I came to the side-gate of the park. It's one of those that clang shut. For some reason I held on to it, so it closed silently.

I started to make my way between the bushes on the bank and then I heard shouting. I stopped. I crouched down and looked across to the football lawn where the noise was coming from.

Clouds moved away from the moon and the guys were lit up. I could see them clearly.

It was The Death Mask Gang. They were in a circle around two guys. One was the gang leader Kimo. The other was Frederick. I knew him. He sometimes played football with us at break. He was twelve, a year older than me.

The other day he told me he was doing the tests to get in the gang. I asked him," Why man?" Then the end of break bell rang and he was gone.

The shouting got louder and angrier. I heard Kimo shout, "Come on. I will fight you!"

Frederick didn't stand a chance. He was five years younger and half the size of Kimo. But Kimo started hitting him. Frederick punched back fast and furiously but Kimo's punches were much heavier and he was soon on the ground.

He lay there. They all just stood around. I thought maybe he's not too badly hurt.

Then he was suddenly on his feet and aiming a flying kick where it hurts.

Kimo screamed and doubled up. When he stood straight again a blade flashed in the moonlight. He ran at Frederick.

The gang shouted at him "No Kimo! No don't do it Kimo."

But he stabbed and stabbed and stabbed. It seemed like hundreds of times.

I heard, "What have you done man! He's dead! He's dead! What have you done!"

Suddenly they were all running towards me. I kept so still. My heart was beating fast and loud.

They were in such a panic to get away they didn't know I was there. I heard the side-gate clang.

I moved a bit and looked over to the lawn. One of the gang was still there. He was looking at Frederick. I think he was seeing if he could be helped. He stood back and bent his head. It looked like he was praying. Then he was running my way. I froze but as he ran past I heard a sneeze. It was me.

He stopped. He turned and looked hard at me. He said, "I know you. You're Mikey. I know where you live."

He said, "What are you doing here?"

I tried to sound normal but I squeaked a bit, "I came to get my blazer. I left it under a tree."

In a low and serious voice he asked "Did you see what happened?"

My heart was pumping so hard I was thinking I might just faint or even die. "What do you mean? I just came to get my blazer."

He growled, "Then why were you hiding? You did see what happened didn't you?"

I started to cry.

He said, "Go get your blazer and go home."

I said, "Now?"

He said, "I said go didn't I?"

I started to run towards the lawn.

He shouted, "Stop!"

I stopped and turned to face him.

He said, "If you ever speak a word about this it will be the end of you."

And he made a cut-throat sign with his finger across his neck.

Then he ran off and I heard the side-gate clang before I started running again.

When I got to the lawn, I knew I had to go to Frederick. I went up to him slowly. I was so scared.

He was such a mess. I can see him now. But he was so bad I don't want to think about it.

I just had to make sure. I called his name, "Frederick, Frederick, talk to me man." The silence that came back was like a deep dark hole. I felt his neck for a pulse like mum taught me. But however much I wanted him to be alive I knew the truth.

I stood up and put my hands together and in my head I said, "God rest your soul amen."

Then I ran to get my blazer. It was shining light blue under the tree. I snatched it up and ran for the main gates.

I knew they would be locked but I've climbed them before. They are tall bar gates with curly spikes at the top painted gold.

I looked around. No-one in sight. I bundled my blazer up and threw it over. It landed neatly on the pavement. Then I climbed up, first half-way, then a push to the top, then over the top to half-way down, then a drop to the pavement.

I got my blazer and started to run for home but two policemen were walking towards me. I stopped for a second then turned and ran the other way.

They shouted," Stop!"

I stopped and turned back around.

One asked, "Why are you out so late?"

I opened my mouth to answer but nothing would

come out. I held out my blazer and pointed to the park. They understood what I was telling them.

One of them crouched down and looked at me properly; he said, "You show us the way now and we'll walk you home".

They were very kind.

Those two kind policemen were back at my home the next day asking me about what I saw. I still couldn't speak but I wrote everything down and when they asked questions I nodded or shook my head or wrote my answers.

Now my family has been taken to what they call a "safe house". It's somewhere secret where the gang can't get them.

I am being sent somewhere far away. They say it will be fun and good for me.

I want Kimo to be punished for what he did.

Right now it's me and my family who are being punished.

# GEORGE

*It's been a very long journey through the night. I've had a lot of time to think my sad angry mixed- up thoughts. Too much time.*

*I wake up as I feel the train slowing down. The sun is trying to rise in a mean grey landscape.*

*Unusually for my new self I am quite calm. I'm just fifteen but I feel ancient. The trouble is that my emotions could crowd in on me at any time. How am I going to get through six weeks in the back of beyond's bum without my rage erupting?*

*I need to remember those anger-management strategies right now before I make myself look a complete arse on minute one of day one.*

*Breathe deeply for ten breaths, now slowly repeat my calming words, "Swimming in the sea, swimming in the sea, swimming in the sea..."*

*Next, visualisation. I have to imagine that I am lying under a golden autumn tree. Every now and then a shining leaf flutters down and I hold out my hand to catch it.*

\*\*\*

The train pulls into the tiny station of Lochair, brakes hissing. I feel a leap of excitement and forget my tiredness. The passwords I've been given for my safety come into my head, "Welcome to Bonnie Scotland."

I get up and stretch my arms and legs before lifting

my suitcase down from the luggage rack and putting on my backpack.

Going forward I see just one figure on the platform, a tall man with bright ginger hair and beard. Our eyes meet as he opens the carriage door.

"Hello George, I'm John. Here, let me take that suitcase for ye'." He smiles and his light- blue eyes twinkle.

"Welcome to Bonnie Scotland!"

"Thanks." I manage to croak. My voice sounds strange and I realise that I haven't spoken to anyone for about twelve hours. Apart from thanking the ticket guy when he passed my ticket back.

"Right then George - let's get ye' to a wee bit o' civilisation."

John carries my suitcase. The ground is too rough and stony for its delicate city wheels.

As we make our way to a mud-spattered Land-Rover I notice that right across the whole wide sweep of land there's not a single other person or building in sight. I stop and take a deep breath of the cool clear air and for a moment I feel dizzy with exhilaration and excitement.

John opens the rear door of the Land-Rover and there's a flash of black and white as a dog springs out, making me jump a bit.

"George meet Trixie. She's a Border Collie, the breed which should make her a very good sheep dog!"

I bend down to stroke this quivering bundle of energy. She yelps as she jumps frantically around me. At last she settles and I stroke her silky head.

Looking into her dark intelligent eyes I feel like I've just made a friend for life.

The three of us climb into the vehicle. It smells of wet turf, diesel, and dog. I wriggle comfortably into the worn red leather bench seat then search for the seatbelt. I clunk the clasp shut then John looks across at me. " Ready for the off George?"

I nod and smile.  It feels like he can't wait to go as he starts the heavy noisy old engine and energetically puts it into gear; there's even a bit of wheel spin on the loose sandy gravel but he soon pushes his strong frame back into the seat and settles down to a more relaxed pace.

Pointed ears pricked forward, eyes intent on the sights ahead, Trixie sits between John and me as we travel across the brown and purple moor.

Curly-horned shaggy-coated sheep and groups of deep brown wide-faced Highland cattle look up lazily from their grazing to watch us rumble by.

"The animals are our only neighbours, George. They're great; they keep the lawns neat and never complain."

I laugh, "We have good neighbours too; on one side they're deaf and on the other side there's a massive noisy family so we all get on all right."

I feel a pang of homesickness as I think about them.

John breaks into my thoughts. "Look now George, can ye' see Summerlands away over there?"

Looking far into the distance I make out a low white building. We draw nearer and suddenly a brilliant shaft of silver sunlight breaks through the grey cloud and shines down only on Summerlands.

The Land Rover scrunches to a halt on the gravel. I struggle a bit with the clunky metal door mechanism then, taking a deep breath of relief, I climb out slowly. Trixie leaps up to greet me as if I'm an old friend she hasn't seen for ages!

John has already retrieved my luggage from the boot. He passes me my rucksack. "Okay George, come and meet Maggie."

We go through an open door into a kind of conservatory, "Maggie we're back," he calls as I become happily aware of a delicious warm waft of baking.

A cheerful voice shouts back," Hi John, you were quick! That train must've been exactly on time!"

The wall sides of the room are lined with coat pegs, many of which have hard-core rain-jackets and anoraks hanging on them. Walking boots, wellies, and well-worn trainers in different sizes occupy some of the spaces in the white metal racks that take up most of the floor. There's a very familiar smell about this space. I know, it's the P.E. changing rooms at school. Regret creeps into my mind.

"We call this the boot-room George." John is sitting on one of the benches and pulling his hiking boots off, "When ye get tae know what the weather can be like up here ye'll know why we make a habit of leaving all our outdoor stuff in here."

I follow his example. Wow! What a pleasure to get my hot sweaty trainers off; placing them on a rack I notice they're a bit stinky. I open them up to let them air like my mum always insists on.

"We'll leave your bags here George and I'll show ye to your room when we've said hello to Maggie. By that smell I reckon she's still doing the baking."

I follow John down a long hallway to the kitchen. He holds the door open for me. I go in and stand there, amazed.

"My! Ye've been busy!"

The long table is full of pies, tarts and cakes of all shapes and sizes, each one looking perfect and delicious.

"We're going to have a house full of young people soon and what better excuse could there be for me to indulge in my absolute favourite hobby?"        Now she looks me firmly in the eye," Ye must be George!  I've been looking forward to meeting ye. How are ye?"

She carefully places the latest pie from the oven on a cooling rack, takes off her oven gloves, turns off the oven, wipes her hands on her apron and shakes my hand warmly.

This is all looking so much better than I'd imagined.

"I'm good thanks. How are you?"

"Very well thank ye George."

She smiles and her big green eyes crinkle at the sides. Her long black hair is tied in a ponytail. It suddenly dawns on me that she is very pretty. And fairly tall.

"Now George, ye must be thirsty. What can I get ye tae drink?"

"Could I have a cup of tea please, quite strong no sugar."

I hope that didn't sound rude, but I really need a proper cup of tea.

Maggie smiles broadly, "That's a heartfelt request George, sounds like ye could do with one of our extra- large mugs. Ye can take it tae your room and have it whilst ye freshen up." Her gentle voice is a female version of John's, with the same lilting accent. Being used to loud North London voices I'm already learning to listen more carefully.

The kettle boils fast and Maggie carefully hands me a huge mug of steaming golden tea, "There ye go George, enjoy!"

"John would ye show George tae his room now please?"

"Ready George?" John raises his eyebrows questioningly at me.

"Yes, thanks," I nod and smile, "Now I've got my tea I'll be fine."

"Now there's a man after my own heart! Follow me!"

John leads me back down the hallway to a door just near the boot room. It has my name on it, on a card in one of those little slot things; George McGlade.

"Your bags are just there George. See ye when ye're ready... take your time...are ye sure ye're okay?"

He looks me in the eye and I see real concern there...when people do that it always makes me feel like crying.

"Yes thanks, I'm fine."

"Alright then I'll leave ye to it."

I watch him walk back down the hall to the kitchen. As the door closes behind him, I feel the floor sinking under my feet. That feeling of desperate sadness like the whole world has moved on and left me on my own.

I go to open the door but the lever handle's stiff. I have to put my mug down on the floor and push the door at the same time as holding the handle down. I push my bags into the room with my foot.

It's such a relief that the room actually looks really good.  I am irresistibly drawn to the bed which is lovely and big. It has a fantastically puffy white-covered duvet. It's like a fine-weather cloud.

Gratefully I fall on to it and lie flat on my back surveying my new space; wood floor with two blue rugs, a window with blue curtains and a view over never-ending moorland. The furniture's made of light wood. I think it's pine. There's a wardrobe, a tall chest of drawers, a desk with loads of paper and pens on top and an office style lamp. There's a book-case too, complete with enough books to last me at least ten years. I'll look at them later.

Better use my bathroom now. I look in the mirror to brush my teeth. I'm surprised to see that I look pretty much the same as I did yesterday; I 'm not vain or anything but I think my face is okay. I have quite a big nose, but I think it just misses being too big; my eyes are a kind of dark green and I have long dark eyelashes. Mum always says they're wasted on a boy, (cringe!). My hair is brown thick and wavy, and beginning to get a bit longer because I don't get it cut over the summer. I'm an all right height, kind of medium, and slim; well maybe a bit skinny right now...

I pick up my empty mug and head down the narrow hall to the kitchen. I knock on the door and open it slowly. "Come and join us George." Maggie points to my seat at the long pine table. "Ye must be starving!"

We eat piles of cheese toasties with ketchup and it's all washed down with never- ending tea from a huge brown teapot.

I didn't realise I was so hungry and now I 'm beginning to feel very full-up and sleepy.

I feel my eyes refusing to stay open. I start to rub them.

"Come on George!" John speaks just as I'm about to give up the struggle to stay awake.

"Trixie and I'll show you around the neighbourhood."

The dog scurries around frantically and yelps until the door is opened. Now she shoots off like a bullet from a gun.

I take a deep breath of that fresh sweet air, blink in the bright white daylight, and forget all about being tired.

"D'ye like walking George?"

"I used to love it, with my mum and dad"

I say the words without thinking and immediately want to take them back. I hope he didn't hear.

We soon settle to a steady pace. I notice that the sky has changed completely from a dull all-over grey to a deep seamless blue.

"George, look up there!" Wheeling high above us is a bird with a massive wingspan. The wings are strangely rectangular. It has a broad fan-shaped tail which assists its effortless progress across the sky.

"It's a golden eagle George."

I can't speak; my heart is soaring with the bird as it plays on the winds. I feel as though time is standing still. I feel for a moment that anything is possible.

Trixie has raced ahead of us whilst we stand in awe but now she comes scooting back, yapping impatiently. John bends down and rubs her ears, "All right Trix, we're coming."

We walk on in silence and I'm shocked when I realise that it's not the sullen angry silence I've been inflicting on people lately. It's a peaceful understanding kind of silence, like you might share with your best mate.

"Look over there George. Can ye see that wee building in the distance? "

I follow his eye -line and see some structures that look man-made.

"Yes, yes I can."

"Well that, is our famous ruined croft!

A croft. That's something I know a bit about. We did about crofting in Year 7.

"Why is it famous John?"

"Good question George. And the answer might surprise you. It's because of the tales of sightings of ghosts there. Almost any local you talk to will have seen what they think to be ghosts. Or know somebody who has.

"What do they look like? What do they do? Have you seen them?"

"I would like to say definitely yes, George. The truth is I think I might have. But it was one of those misty days when a tree can look like a giraffe and a bush can look like an elephant. And we don't expect to see many of those around here!"

"That's amazing! What do the ghosts look like?"

"Some say they saw wee bairns, others talk about highland warriors. But it would seem that most of the sightings have been of normal crofters from way back in the past, going about their daily work in a peaceful way."

"Do you think I will get a chance to see them John?"

"Aye George, if they do exist, you will have as much chance as anybody.

I often walk the dog there but we're still quite a way off it. But hey, there'll be plenty o' time for ye t'explore while ye're here. I think it's time to turn around and go back now. I reckon supper'll be ready when we walk in the door."

This is a relief to me because I've just become aware of a massive weariness. And to my surprise I'm feeling quite hungry as well.

We walk back the way we came. It seems to take quite a long time but there again I don't have much idea of time now. I never wear a watch and my mobile phone has been "locked away for safe keeping".  My anger threatened to get the better of me when they told me about that particular "house-rule" but I took some deep breaths and waited for the moment to pass. Now I'm beginning to understand that up here with no buses, trains, or television, time has little significance anyway.

The smell of supper cooking greets and pulls us from what seems a long way from base. I suddenly feel extremely hungry and my pace quickens.

"Race you George!"

I find myself running as fast as I can but John goes ahead; I manage to catch up just as we reach the house.

We're both out of breath and laughing as we take our

shoes off and Trixie jumps around and yaps excitedly.

We sit at the kitchen table. Our places are set so that we're all together at one end; John and Maggie are opposite me so we make a triangle. A low hanging light shines a warm glowing circle over our heads. When no one's speaking we can hear only the ticking of the large wood-framed kitchen clock on the chimney breast.

Cheesy-topped cottage pie with thick gravy, carrot, peas and crusty bread . . . it's actually my favourite meal . . .how did they know? Was it put down on a form somewhere?

"What's it like where ye live George?" Maggie asks between mouthfuls.

I quickly chew and swallow. "I live in North London," I reply, picturing my house in my head. "It's quite nice; well it's home. Mum and Dad bought it when they were expecting me. They renovated it together. It's the only house I've ever lived in. Dad wasn't a builder but my Granddad is and he helped Dad do the improvements. My Mum works as a doctor's receptionist but she should probably be an interior designer really. She's made the inside of the house beautiful."

I stop talking, realising that this is the most I've talked to anyone, (apart from Mum), about anything since Dad went. Every other time tears have come, and that's made me angry, so I've been doing a lot of storming out.

Again, the big brown teapot is full, and I lose count of the refills I have. I think to myself that this is a good feature of being here.

I 'm beginning to go into the kind of trance that comes just before you fall asleep when I realise John's talking about ghosts.

"They say the ruined croft is haunted; one or two of the locals have seen wee bairns in old fashioned clothes and boots, and a teenaged laddie wearin' the kilt. They said that they spoke to them and the bairns dinna hear but the older laddie seemed to know someone was there."

As John begins to talk about "the legend of the feud" in his quiet lilting voice I can feel myself beginning to drift off again, "Mmmmm," I hear my voice saying, and my head jerks up...I've fallen asleep...literally nodded off. How embarrassing!

I quickly stand up to stop it happening again and then realise I haven't excused myself - heck this is getting worse - so I say in a strange rushed way, "That was a great meal, thanks- would you excuse me please".

I start putting plates together to clear the table...

"Och George don't ye be worrying ye'self aboot that noo." Maggie says softly, interrupting my frantic activity.

"Get ye'self to bed."

I feel myself smiling gratefully. I look up. "Okay, thank you."

"Goodnight Maggie, goodnight John."

"Goodnight George."

Their voices remind me of the breeze blowing gently over the heather.

I fumble my way to my room, throw off my clothes and burrow into the crisp white covers. For the first time since Dad went, I have no trouble settling and I am soon deeply asleep.

# THE CROFT

*I feel the need to get out, to escape.*

*I yank my bedroom door open and run to the outside door. Desperately I struggle with the lock. When I finally manage to pull the door back a solid wall of fog gets in the way of freedom. I shout out and Trixie starts yapping loudly. John and Maggie come and catch me, each taking hold of one of my arms. I shout again and then wake in a sweat, covers kicked to the floor.*

***

Controlling my panic with deep breaths I look around and gradually remember where I am.

I grab the bottle of water from my bedside table and drink all of it. Now I'm wide awake. I know I will probably never be able to get back to sleep again so I think I might as well write the letter home which I've been told by John and Maggie, is one of the flipping "rules of the house".

*Dear Mum,*

*Why have you sent me here? It's weird and strange and miles from anywhere. I hate it. It smells like Nan's house, all musty and cleaning chemicals. Everything's bare and shiny; the floors are wood, the walls are half wood and half white-painted bricks.*

*Why am I here?*

*The people who run this place are very quiet, a man and a*

*woman. They are probably only about twenty-four or twenty-five but they don't act like it. They act like oldies! Why would normal young people want to live here?*

*There is NOTHING here. All there is for miles and miles is reddish-brown earth with patches of purple; then far away there are mountains.*

*I have never liked the idea of mountains. I don't think they're beautiful. I've never wanted to climb them. They are POINTLESS.*

*Mum, what am I going to do here for six weeks? Why didn't you want me to go to Australia to visit Auntie Claire with you?*

*I feel trapped like I'm in a prison even though the doors are always open. Do you think I'm mental or something? I do feel very, very angry, but that's because you've sent me here.*

*I'm fifteen Mum, did you forget? There are no computers and my 'phone has been locked away by John and Maggie. They said it was one of the "rules of the house."*

*I nearly cried when I had to give my 'phone up. What have you done to me?*

*I don't even know why I'm writing this stupid letter. You probably won't even bother to read it.*

*I thought you needed me.*

*You kept saying that you relied on me; that you would fall apart without me. How come that suddenly changed? One minute, life wouldn't be worth living if I wasn't there. Next minute, "Bye son, have a good time."*

*Dismissed without hesitation. Suddenly not needed any more. Abandoned twice! It feels like there must be something about me that drives people away, or makes them send me away.*

*Missing you Mum,*

*Your abandoned son,*

*George.*

*P.S. I'm on my own here until the next victim arrives. It's a girl. I need my mates Mum, not some stupid girl.*

\*\*\*

I must have fallen back to sleep somehow because the next thing I'm aware of is some gentle but insistent knocking on my door. "Good morning George, are ye awake yet? Breakfast is in ten minutes!"

"Thank you, John," I manage to mutter, "Yes, I'm wide awake, I'll just have a quick shower and I'll be there."

Whilst I get ready, I wonder if they heard me shout out in the night. I'm really hoping not. I feel very hungry again. I haven't wanted to eat like this for ages. I've been eating only because I had to. I follow my nose to the kitchen.

"Good morning George, did ye sleep well?" Maggie

turns from the cooker where bacon and sausages are sizzling alongside eggs and tomatoes in an enormous frying pan.

"Yes, thank you, very well." Just a little polite white lie. Thank goodness it looks like they didn't hear me shouting out in my dream.

Breakfast is very good. Before the fry- up, fruit juice and porridge, following the fry-up, toast and marmalade, all washed down with multiple mugs of tea from that bottomless teapot.

I'm helping to clear the table when John asks me if I'd like to take Trixie out on my own. I try not to sound too excited about the offer, "Yes, that'd be good, thanks." Inwardly I'm ecstatic. I've always wanted a dog and Trixie is amazing!

It's absolutely chucking it down with rain, but John finds me an anorak and some wellies in the boot-room. "If we didna' go out in the rain up here George," he laughs, "We wouldna' get out very much!"
I wouldn't be seen dead in this outfit in my own neighbourhood but I know I'm unlikely to come across anyone at all around here. And definitely not anyone I know. Maggie comes through with a pack of sandwiches and a bottle of water which I put in the inside pockets of the anorak.
John passes me Trixie's lead;" Here, put this in your pocket, just in case; ye most likely won't need it. I suggest ye head for the ruined croft that I pointed out yesterday. It's an interesting spot. Just go in the opposite direction to the

mountains.  Trixie often goes there with me so she'll take ye, and don't worry if she goes off, she always finds her way home."

Tail wagging furiously, Trixie's waiting by the door. John opens it and she practically flies out. And I fly after her. I haven't run out of a door like that since I was about eight. Through net curtains of rain, I see Trixie far ahead. She's loving it, running on and then barking whilst waiting for me, or running back to round me up, like a proper sheepdog.

With the uneven ground getting wetter and heavier by the second I soon slow down to a squelchy walk; I'm having to almost pull up my feet up for each step.

* * *

After an hour or so I stand still and look all around me. The massive sky is clearing; great swathes of grey cloud sweep away and reveal a fantastic blue. The sun is warming my head and making the purple heather and green grass sparkle. And there's that ultimate completely best scent in the world which is made by sun on wet turf.

An enormous smile grows across my face. I take a deep breath, throw my head back and scream.

Now I've stopped walking, I notice that my legs are aching. Trixie seems to be slowing down a bit as well. I'm tempted to turn around and go back but I soon talk myself out of that idea with two thoughts; one, by the way he spoke about it John expects me to make it to the croft, two, I'm having an amazing day out in the wilds with the best walking companion I could ever get.

She's walking by my side now. "I'm loving this walk Trixie. You're so lucky to live here. Even the rain's good; I mean it's proper rain, total wetness, and it's made me feel different. This boggy ground's a bit of a pain though. I suppose it doesn't affect you so much with your four feet."

I would never have thought somewhere so empty and silent could give me such a buzz. I feel high on freedom! "Dad would have loved it Trix." This thought takes me back to my usual never- ending circle. I find myself telling Trixie all about it.

"After Dad went, home didn't feel like home anymore but Mum and I had to carry on and try to live normal lives. We felt as though we would lose each other as well if we ever let go. We clung tightly together and slowly, so slowly, got ourselves together. We made new routines to lean on, texting each other at set times during the day, making sure to have the kettle on if we were first home . . . Trixie, I used to feel so sad and yet so proud when Mum used to say that I was her rock and she didn't know what she would do without me.

I've been thinking loads about all this before and getting so angry I scared myself. Who wouldn't get angry? When basically I've been lied to. She told me that she couldn't have managed without me. Then sent me away! What was all that about? I just don't understand."

I take some deep breaths, ten deep breaths, concentrating on them, as per the counselling. In through the nose, slowly, deeply. Out through the mouth, exhaling fully, emptying my lungs, and getting rid of my anger at the same time. Like nearly always the method works. I feel calm.

I put my hands behind my head and kind of roughly scratch my scalp as I look all around me and take in the wild beauty of the moor. I look down and Trixie looks up into my eyes. It feels like she's seeing right into my heart. Then she whimpers and quivers and jumps around in circles because she's had enough of waiting for me.

I feel great now, relaxed and excited that I'm discovering new stuff. I feel for the first time in ages that Christmas-stocking anticipation. When you feel with your feet to see if Father Christmas has been, making the tension last by trying to work out with your toes what might be in there, and finally succumbing to your thrill of curiosity and sheer happiness when you sit up and grab the stocking, look at it , and start to guess again what each lovingly-wrapped package contains.

At last I see the outline of a small building, irregular in shape; this must be the croft. Forgetting my tired legs and the mud-heavy wellies, I start running towards it; Trixie's well excited about the change of pace and jumps around my feet as if she wants me to trip over. She keeps yapping and squealing until we reach our destination.

I stand in awe for a moment. This place exudes some kind of power, something mystical. I think I would almost be surprised if it *wasn't* haunted.

After taking a huge deep breath I walk round the ruins. The building is constructed from large thick white stones, and even though most of it has fallen down, it keeps within it a massive dignity. There are four external walls, mostly standing to my waist level, although one of them is high enough for a window space to be discernible. My favourite feature is the chimney stack which has a graceful kind of curve and seems to have lost hardly any height over the years.

I step over a line of thick white stone bricks that mark a doorway. There is a warmth and light here that envelop me. An overwhelming sense of peace and security force me to be still for maybe seconds, maybe minutes, whilst I absorb it all. The floor of the croft has room sections marked by dark wooden beams. How come they haven't completely rotted away?  The kitchen has a large fireplace and amazingly there are also the remains of a wooden kitchen dresser. It would once have been practically identical to the one Dad got for Mum.  It was what she needed to put the final touch to her dream cottage-style kitchen. They were so full of joy on the day that piece of furniture arrived, not knowing that within months everything would change. For a moment I feel a sharp pain of grief.

The sun's rays are now intense and the wetness of the rain is steaming off me and everything around me, including Trixie, who shakes herself energetically, drinks from a puddle and then flops down next to the fireplace for a sleep. I'm thinking that looks like a brilliant idea. I take off my coat, give it a shake, arrange it on the ground next to the dog and curl in the foetal position like I always do. Safety and warmth embrace me like a parent cuddling a child...

***

*The fire's glowing brightly and an oil lamp lights the faces of the family sitting around the long pine table. They're eating a steaming hot stew from earthenware bowls.  The family pass a brown loaf around the table. Each person carefully tears off a chunk before giving it to the next. I hear them chatting; two or three quiet conversations are going on...*

*The youngest grandson, about eight with ginger hair and freckles on his little snub nose, is talking earnestly to the grandfather who sits at the head of the table.*

*The grandfather has a strong face with thick white eyebrows, beard and hair. He's listening to the boy with great concentration.*

*At the opposite end of the table the grandmother sits up very straight. She has fading auburn hair which is worn in a round bun, and curly tendrils frame her gentle face.*

*The mother, who is sitting opposite her husband at the long side of the table, has pale skin and jet-black hair done in a single long plait. She looks calm and content, a gentle smile plays on her face as she watches her children. She is actually beautiful in what Mum would call "a striking way".*

*Next to her sits the youngest child, a girl of about four with unbelievably bright red hair, gabbling animatedly to her sister, who is sitting next to her. This girl is about six and has black hair like her mother. The two children are both dressed in grey long-sleeved dresses with white pinafores over the top.*

*Their father is another red-haired member of the family with matching beard, moustache and eyebrows. Although he's sitting down, I can see that he's tall and strongly built; he looks like a Viking! Deeply engaged in conversation with him is the eldest son; about my age, with the same colouring as his father, his red hair is wild and his green eyes flash with enthusiasm as he speaks. This boy is dressed the same as his father and grandfather, in a rough grey shirt with baggy sleeves, a sheepskin waistcoat, and a longish kilt which is not made of tartan but a rough looking fabric in a brownish colour. All of the family wear sturdy loose- fitting leather boots.*

*Under the table near the feet and legs lies a border collie which looks identical to Trixie. Every now and then I see a little hand reaching down to offer a small piece of bread or meat which is gently snuffled up.*

*The mother rises now and fetches a big brown teapot from which she serves the adults. The children are given milk from the jug. The family drinks in silence. Now everyone looks expectantly at Grandfather, who clears his throat. They all close their eyes and he says, "Thankyou Father for our loved ones and the food we have shared."*

*"Mother, may we get down now please?" The youngest child is beginning to climb off her chair already.*

*The mother laughs, "Of course ye may and ye other wee'uns; ye can start clearin' the table for me if ye would be sae kind."*

*"Mother, thank you for the fine meal; may I go and tend to the animals now?" The older boy is rising from his seat.*

*"Yes of course, son." He stops by the door to get his hat from the peg. As he lifts the latch he turns slightly to the side and his eyes look straight into mine. He scratches his head in seeming disbelief, then puts on his hat and goes to do his evening chores.*

*The adults sit in the gentle lamplight and I hear the soft waves of their quiet conversation as the evening turns to night.*

***

I wake shivering and stand up stiffly, then bend down to pick up my coat which I shake roughly and put on. I stretch my arms and legs before stepping over the threshold stones and out of the croft. When I feel the sandwiches in the zip-pocket my heart skips a beat. They're a bit squashed and soggy but they fill my stomach very nicely. I down the bottle of water as well. Then I look round for Trixie. I can't see her! "Trixie! Trixie! come on girl, where are you? It's home time now, come on!

I call again and again. It feels like she's gone forever and the sun is going down so fast. I try the ear-splitting finger and thumb whistle that Dad taught me, but she still doesn't come. . .

I keep on and on shouting and whistling 'til my throat is sore and I've run out of puff.

Still she doesn't come. Abandoned again! I feel savage. I throw myself to the ground and kick and scream as loud as I can. I shout and swear with the worst words I know. I stand up and look for rocks which I snatch up and hurl, each one farther than the last.

Exhausted I dive to the ground in the fading light and cry and cry buckets of tears I didn't know I had. And whilst I lie here bawling like a giant baby Trixie comes back and talks to me in a whimper, licking my face and washing my tears away.

"Trixie you're amazing," I hug my new best friend, burying my face in her wet-dog smelling hair and wondering how she knows so well how to comfort me.

Starlight is taking over from sunlight as the last of the purples, pinks, and yellows drain reluctantly from the sky. There are more stars than I have ever seen before, shining brighter than diamonds, a sharper and more thrilling light than I could ever have imagined. Why didn't anybody tell me? I guess there are some things you just have to find out for yourself.

The walk back seems much shorter than the walk out. Trixie kind of slinks beside me in that classic sheepdog position. Lights not as bright as the stars but just as welcome show me I'm nearly home.

# SMIDGIN

The sound of tyres scrunching on gravel rouses me from a deep sleep; then the gentle thud of a car door closing, followed by the more robust bang of a second one, make sure that I'm completely awake.

I know it's not the Land Rover because I would recognise the clunk, and I'm curious. There haven't been any visitors at all since I arrived, and with new-found nosiness I want to see who this is. I creep into the hall and look through the glass of the boot-room.

A woman of about thirty I should think, dressed in jeans and a sweatshirt, is speaking with John and Maggie whilst a girl of about ten looks on. Well I say girl because she definitely is but she's dressed in a very a tomboyish way.  She has pale skin, I can see that from here, and her little nose has freckles on it. Her short black hair is shiny and her eyes are a very bright blue. Skinny jeans, a red hooped tee-shirt and white trainers complete her Dennis the Menace look.

Now the woman shakes hands with the adults, gives the girl a brief hug, climbs into her car and, with a cheerful beep of the horn, drives off.

John picks up the girl's suitcase and I rush back to my room before they all come inside.

I take my time showering and dressing before I go for breakfast, figuring that they'll need to spend some time settling "Dennis the Menace" in, without me on the scene.

Eventually I smell that magical aroma of a full English, or should I say full Scottish, breakfast, and I take it as my cue to appear.

As I approach the kitchen, I hear a bloodcurdling scream.

"No!  You can bloody well not have my mobile phone! It's mine; me social worker bought it for me! I need it to talk to me mam!"

Trixie joins me outside the closed kitchen door whilst I wait for a lull in the conflict. I can hear John speaking in a low calming voice but I can't hear what he's saying.  After a few minutes of quiet I knock gently on the door and he calls me in.

"Come on in George, breakfast is good and ready!"

The new girl is sitting at the breakfast table ferociously tucking into egg and bacon; she looks up briefly and acknowledges my presence with a full-mouthed nod. I nod back. Maggie breaks into the noisy eating sounds,

" Good morning George. Come on over and meet Jasmine."

"It's not Jasmine!" the girl protests, spitting half-chewed food all over the place, "It's Smidgin! I told you before!"

 I'm thinking blimey this new arrival could liven things up around here; I hold out my hand and we shake, a sticky, delicate shake. It is a moment of peace.

But all hell breaks loose when Trixie pads along, tail

wagging in a friendly way, to greet Smidgin. Another bloodcurdling scream!  Trixie starts yapping; Smidgin jumps up and stands on her chair, face as white as the plate she's clutching. She's sobbing hysterically, "Please! Please! Please! Get that bloody thing away from me!"

The situation has erupted so rapidly that we're all a bit dazed by it but after a few seconds John takes control, "There now Smidgin it's all right, the dog willna harm ye. She's a wee bit excited that's all. Come on now Trixie, stop that dreadful noise!"

Smidgin is still really pale and shaking violently. John speaks so quietly it's practically a whisper, "George would ye mind taking Trixie out for a wee while so we can reassure this poor lassie that she's really not in any danger."

I don't need asking twice. I'll never tire of Trixie and the great outdoors.

*** 

It's suppertime and it looks like the dog problem has been sorted out because Smidgin and Trixie are in the same room, fairly near to each other, and there's no screaming or barking going on. Phew!

The food's not quite ready but the table's laid, (I did it, it was one of my duties for the day), and Smidgin and I are enjoying a pre-dinner drink (tea) and some chunks of bread and butter. My well-brought-up manners kick in and I realise that I must at least try to have a conversation with my new acquaintance, "What do you think of our holiday home then Smidgin?" I find to my alarm that I sound like a well-meaning uncle or something. But Smidgin doesn't seem to notice. Her eyes light up.

"I completely totally love it!  I want to stay here forever and ever, providin' me mam can stay as well of course."

"What's your best thing so far?"

"I love everything, me room, me bed, the food's outstandin', just everything!"

"Are you okay with the dog now?"

"Yeah well, it was a bit of a shock like, I didn't know she was there, and the dogs that I've known before 'aven't been that friendly like. I'm gettin' used to the idea of 'avin 'er around now"

"For me the dog is the best thing about this place, she's a brilliant dog, I . . ."

I tail off, as I realise I'm beginning to sound a bit too enthusiastic, "Where are you from Smidgin?"

"Liverpool me. I'm a scouser. Warrabout you?"

"I'm from London. I suppose I'm a Londoner."

"Right yous two," Maggie is carrying a massive golden pie, "This is very hot so don't burn your fingers."

Maggie brings the veggies, mashed potato, and gravy to the table and then calls John. He comes in quietly as she starts to dish up.

"Now then Smidgin, what can I help you to? There's

steak pie, mashed potato, broccoli, and carrots. Ooh, and gravy of course."

"I'd like a lorrov everything if I'm allowed please." Smidgin's eyes suddenly look enormous.

"Of course you're allowed. There's much more than enough for all of us."

Maggie dishes up a man- sized meal. "Tuck in Smidgin!"

Smidgin just stares at the plate placed before her, with an expression of unbelieving joy. Now she sniffs each different food, starting with the potatoes, next the carrots and broccoli and finishing with the pie.

Picking up a piece of carrot with her fingers Smidgin suddenly changes up to fifth gear. With a look of fierce concentration she loads food into her deceptively tiny mouth as if she hasn't eaten for months and does not want to miss out on this opportunity by being too slow.

I can't help watching as she crams the food in, now using both hands, grabbing with one as she puts food in with the other. There's a lot of food stuck to her face when, within a few minutes, her plate is empty. But she doesn't leave it there; she wipes it off with her fingers and solemnly licks them clean. After cleaning  her plate in the same way she looks up, "Wha're are you friggin starin' at?"

I feel my face going red, "Sorry. I'm really sorry. That was just the fastest eating I've ever seen."

"Wha're of it? Is it any of your friggin' business?"

Oops! I've got myself into a bit of a hole! Whilst I

struggle to think of an answer to get me out of it, Maggie intervenes, thank goodness.

"Would ye like some more Smidgin? Or d'ye want to leave a wee space in your tummy for some pudding?"

Immediately forgetting about our conflict Smidgin turns to Maggie, "Coo yeah ta, and I always have space for puddin'!"

As Maggie places a smaller second helping in front of Smidgin the mood in the room relaxes and I try to make my sigh of relief a quiet one.

The food's good and the company's good. We talk about everything from pop groups to football teams and favourite foods to favourite animals.

I can't believe it when Smidgin has seconds of golden syrup sponge and custard but this time I manage not to stare as she does the magical disappearing food trick.

Having finished the last of the tea from the big brown pot I volunteer to wash up.

John's quick to accept, "Well that's an offer we canna refuse George. Ye know where everything is don't ye?"

"Yes I think so. I'll soon find out by looking anyway."

"I'll 'elp yer!" Smidgin pipes up.

I throw a tea towel at her and as we start clearing the table John and Maggie leave the room. We make a surprisingly good team; Smidgin is as good at clearing the kitchen as she is at clearing her plate and we're soon done.

# GEORGE CONFESSES

We sit at the bare pine table admiring our dazzling handiwork.  Everything's clean and back in its right place; well we had to guess on some things. I feel like getting Smidgin to do a high-five but I manage not to.

Now, with elbows on the table, chin cupped in hands, she regards me seriously, "Georgie, wha're you in for then?"

This takes me by surprise because even if I have felt isolated and kind of trapped, I haven't really felt like I was in prison.

"What d'you mean Smidgin? Do you really think we're in gaol?"

"Well it's as good as isn't it? Are you goin' to tell me then?"

I feel my defences breaking down. She's so direct and although she's kind of wild there's also some innocence and wisdom about her. I take a deep breath.

"I got angry. Badly, scarily angry. I had some fights at school. I deliberately broke some stuff. I got kicked out after I threw a chair at a teacher."

I can hardly believe I'm telling her this, I've been trying to hide it from myself and now I'm telling someone I've only just met.

Smidgin looks astonished, eyes wide, trying to comprehend.

"But you're so posh and rich, wha're 'ave you got to

be angry about?"

For a long silent moment I hesitate. The only person I've talked to about this is my counsellor and it took me months of sitting in silence with him before I said a word. If I tell Smidgin I'll have to start moving towards acceptance and I don't know if I'll ever be ready for that.

I look at her; she's looking searchingly into my eyes.

"I wasn't always angry. I hardly even knew the meaning of the word. I probably didn't realise it at the time, but I think my life was perfect before my dad went."

"Oooooh! So yer dad left yer did he? Did he run off with another woman?"

My eyes close as my anger rises and I feel my mouth stretch wide as I half- scream half-shout, making a noise that seems not to come from me, "Noooooo!"

The horrible brutal sound brings me back to my senses. I look at Smidgin. She's still sitting in her chair but she's turned white and she's shaking with fear. I'm completely gutted to see what my anger has done.

"Smidgin I'm so sorry, I didn't mean to do that. It just came out." My throat tightens and my mouth dries as I try to get the words out.

"My dad...my dad...he, he was badly sick for two years ... and then, then ...then he died... Smidgin I'll catch you later."

I push my chair back clumsily and it clatters to the floor as I make a dash for the door.

I get to my room before the tears come.

*\*\**

I didn't close my curtains last night and the bright early light of the rising sun wakes me up. It is really early. The room clock says four thirty.  Summer daylight hours are longer than at home. They give you more time.

I think about the dream I had in the night. It was about me and mum and dad together, happy on a sunny walk. I 'm surprised to find that I'm still feeling happy thinking about it, instead of the sharp pain of loss that I usually get when I wake from those dreams.

Now Smidgin pops into my head and I immediately feel terrible at the way I scared her. I hope she won't be afraid of me this morning. I really like her; if I were ever to have a sister in my life, I would want one just like her. I wonder what she's "in" for.

A loud knocking rouses me from my thinking.

"George! . . . Georgie. . . Georgie. . . are you awake? It's me-- Smidgin!"

I feel my mouth widening into a huge smile. . . "No, I'm asleep. . . but come in anyway!"

"I've made yer a cup of tea, do yer like it sweet? I've put five sugars in it."

"Thanks Smidgin that's great."

Downing the huge mug of milky tea I find that she wasn't joking about the sugars, it really is sickly sweet but definitely just what I needed.

"Georgie! let's go for a walk."

Smidgin takes the mug back to the kitchen whilst I get my clothes on. I scribble a note to tell John and Maggie where we've gone like I always did for mum then we grab the dog's lead and leap to freedom through the always unlocked door. Trixie races far ahead, delighted with her early run.

"We'll go the way I went on my own the other day if that's okay with you Smidgin."

"Course it is Georgie boy! Where are we goin' ?"

"Towards an old ruin, I reached it before but it's quite a long way so we may not get there this morning."

"Yeah, I don't want to go too far. I'm gettin' a bit hungry like. Tell me about the ruin Georgie"

"Well Smidgin, it's an old croft - that means a kind of small farm in Scotland. There are some still going I think, but not many. There used to be a lot. John said something about the place being haunted but I didn't really hear much because I was falling asleep."

"Oooooh Georgie that sounds too scary, I don't think I want to go there."

She's gone as white as a sheet and I feel stupid for not realising that she might be afraid of the idea of ghosts. She just seems so clever and wise that it's easy to forget how young she is. I definitely won't tell her about the dream I had there.

We amble along in the already warm sunshine. I'm not thinking or worrying about anything, I just feel calmer than I can ever remember.

"George! Georgie, look at tha' enormous bird up there! It's making a screaming sound, worr is it?"

I feel really chuffed that I know this one from walks with mum and dad. I shield my eyes as I look up." That's a buzzard."

Smidgin bursts out laughing, "George mind yer language! Yer may not like that poor bird but there's no need ta call it rude names!"

Now she notices a butterfly and, bending down, creeps after it like a little hunter, "Look George, I've caught it!" Cupped in her delicate white hands is a tiny pale blue butterfly; we both hold our breath as we admire its fragile beauty before Smidgin opens her fingers to let it flutter back to freedom.

She's like a very young child discovering nature for the first time, needing to touch and talk about everything. She is just so cool. Again I think that having a sister like her could only be a good thing.

All of a sudden, she stops still and grabs my arm dramatically," Georgie, this is the best place I have ever been!"

"Smidgin, it's definitely already one of my favourite places as well." To my surprise, my answer, which was meant to be polite and kind, is actually the truth. And although I won't tell her right now, this place has become a whole lot better since she arrived.

We sit on the heather watching the bees, hundreds of them. In this peaceful place the buzzing seems almost noisy.

"What are they doing Georgie?"

"They're collecting a kind of juice called nectar. When they've loaded as much as they can carry, they take it back to the hive to make honey."

Smidgin rests her head on a pillow of heather to watch more closely.

"Oh yeah I see what you mean. Look at this one. . . he's carrying so much he can hardly fly. He looks like me mam when she actually has been to do some shopping, all little spindly sparrer legs on three-inch heels and two big fat bags loaded with food that she can only just manage to lift off the ground."

We laugh, although the image of her mum is kind of a bit sad as well as funny.

Lying on the heather, we drift off into our own thoughts.

Me scaring Smidgin last evening comes into my head. "Smidgin... I want to say sorry for being such an idiot last night. Will you forgive me?"

"Nuttin' ter forgive Georgie boy, it was my fault, me and me big mouth."

Now we fall back into our silence again, soaking up the luscious warm rays of the sun, listening to the humming of the bees and smelling the gentle yet powerful scent of the heather.

"Georgie," Smidgin says quietly, "Georgie, do yer want ter know why I'm here?"

"Only if you want to tell me Smidgin."

She takes a deep breath, looks at me solemnly, and speaks in a grave tone. "It's because I keep breakin' the law."

Studying my face intently to see if I react, she carries on;" I haven't done nuttin' really bad, just a bit of shopliftin'. . . I even showed the stuff to the cashiers on me way out like, and I said thank you and goodbye!"

I just stay calm, showing no emotion, like my counsellor does when I'm talking, or even when I'm silent and he wants to encourage me to "open-up".

"And I've been causing a few traffic accidents like."

This sounds more serious and I probably look a bit shocked.

"But they were only very little accidents. All I did was pretend I was goin' to cross in front of a few cars. They were only movin' slowly so the bangs weren't very big like. Nobody was hurt, Georgie."

I don't know what to say to this and Smidgin seems worried by my silence, "I was bored Georgie. I wanted someone to notice me."

This makes me sad and it makes me think about how different our lives have been. I clear my throat. "Haven't you got any family Smidgin, besides your mum? No dad, or brothers and sisters?"

"Well I know I've got a dad somewhere because he sends me a tenner at Christmas and on me birthday, but I don't know what he looks like or where he lives. I 'ave got me mam, but she's not at home much. So when I get meself into trouble and the police take me home there's never anyone there, so they 'ave to get me social worker; she's called Ann. She's really kind and she always finds me a dead good temporary foster home. That means I get some nice food and a cosy room until me mam comes to get me. I think I've been sent here to give me social worker a rest."

We sit with our own thoughts, feeling the sun on our faces, hearing the lightest of breezes softly moving the heather and gorse.

I'm thinking that Smidgin has never had a dad in her life and she hasn't seen much of her mum either by the sound of it. I had the best dad and I know for sure that my mum will always be there for me.

Smidgin has closed her eyes and is smiling gently. I suddenly feel fiercely protective of her...

The dreamy silence is broken by a loud tummy-rumbling... "Georgie was that you?"

"No it was not! You know it was you!"

Now there's an even louder more insistent sound. We look at each other and burst out laughing. Every time we stop laughing there's a yet funnier sound. Now my stomach replies to hers and we're hysterical with it; we're crying with laughter. Tears stream down our faces and every time we look at each other we just start again.

"Smidgin, Smidge, Smidgin, I, I, think. . . think. . . think we should get back now and feed our poor bellies." I take a deep breath, relieved that I got through the sentence without succumbing to more giggles.

"Good idea Georgie boy!"

I hold out my hands and pull her up to standing. Now we shout for Trixie to come. She bombs over to us and we all head back to base. When we get near, we can, as usual, smell delicious food. We look at each other, shout "Yes!" in unison and start running.

"Hi, we're back!" I call out as we make our way to the kitchen.

Maggie shouts out, "Thought ye'd be hungry by now; were your bellies rumbling?" We're both back to the giggles as we go through the door. Then we stop dead in our tracks. There are two new kids sitting at the table.

"Come and meet Ayesha, and Lloyd," Maggie breaks our stunned silence.

I step towards the girl. I'm unable to take my eyes off her but somehow, I manage to hold out my hand and speak, even if it does come out a bit croaky, "Hi I'm George and this is Smidgin." Smidgin comes forward, hand outstretched, and I realise that I'm still holding Ayesha's cool slender hand. I release it hastily.

"Hello George." I just keep looking at her; about my age, she's very cool. Her long legs stretch out under the table. She has black hair so shiny it has a blue effect like a starling's feathers, massive brown eyes, and what people call a generous mouth, which would look amazing if she smiled. I think she could light up the whole world if she smiled. In fact as I look at her, I forget about everything else in the world.

Maggie calls me back to consciousness, "Right George and Smidgin, now meet Lloyd."

I follow Smidgin to the other side of the table and hold out my hand. "Hi I'm George and this is Smidgin, I expect you heard just now," I joke feebly, "Anyway, very pleased to meet you."

It seems like it's quite an effort for him to slowly reach out and shake each of our hands lightly and briefly; his eye contact is brief and light also. He speaks very quietly as if to himself but I'm pretty sure he says, "Hi, how're you." He has untidy brown hair down to his shoulders and thoughtful grey eyes framed by large black glasses.

His skin is very pale; it looks as if he never goes outside. He's quite tall but he seems to be trying to look smaller because his shoulders are hunched up and his legs are kind of curled round the legs of his chair. Both his thumbs keep moving, as if independently from his brain. Dressed in jeans and an ancient-looking Iron Maiden Tee-shirt, one word sums him up for me at this moment - and that word is geek. I should know because my best friend at home is one!

Formalities complete, Smidgin and I sit at the table and eat for Olympic gold, (Smidgin manages to use a fork... mostly).

"More tea anyone?" I have to offer before I drain the pot into my cup but luckily no-one wants any.

Now Maggie and John excuse themselves and leave the room.

Smidgin gets up and starts clearing the table and putting the sauces, jams, and butter away. I go to the massive white sink and start running the water for the washing up. Now Ayesha joins in helping with the clearing.

She and Smidgin take the blue-checked table-cloth outside to shake the crumbs off. I hear them chanting, "Fold the cloth together be friends forever" and then laughing. It makes me feel sad and happy at the same time because I remember my mum and dad doing that. Only Lloyd is still sitting at the table, head down like he's afraid to move.

Smidgin breaks the deadlock by throwing a tea-towel at him; "Come on Lloyd, why should we have all the fun?" It lands on his head. He doesn't reply but he looks grateful as he slowly removes it, shakes it, and makes his way to the drying-up side of the sink. He dries each item slowly and methodically. Holding each piece up to the light he checks for any smears, tutting and rubbing frantically if he finds one.

We all watch him with bated breath. Smidgin and Ayesha start competing to be first to pick up the finished items and put them away. Lloyd joins in the game in the end, he places the things at the far end of the table then says," Ready, steady, go!"

It gets quite hectic. And very funny. We all end up laughing helplessly in a heap on the floor.

# MIKEY ARRIVES

As the darkness is pushed gently away by the clear white light of the early sun I hear a knock at my door followed by Smidgin's very loud stage whisper, "Georgie, Georgie, I've got a lovely cup of tea for you, can I come in?"

What I would really like is about half an hour more to doze a bit and wake up slowly, but I've already learnt that I can never say no to Smidgin and I don't even want to really.

"Come in Smidgin, good morning!" Carefully she passes my cup of sugar flavoured with milk and a splash of tea. "Thanks Smidgin. Who taught you how to make tea?"

"I taught myself.  Do you like it?"

"It's the best I've ever had!"

"Come on then lazybones, drink it up and get out of bed. Me and Trixie want a walk!"

"All right, all right, can I get dressed first?"

"Course you can! I'll see you at the door in two minutes!"

The rest of the house is silent as we carefully shut the door behind us then run into the cool misty morning. Amazingly everything is fresh and new again, dew sparkles all around us on grass and heather, on the little low trees, and on spiders' webs; it makes each thing it touches like the most precious of jewellery.

The beauty isn't wasted on Smidgin; she's the most observant and appreciative person I've ever met, and she sparkles with it just like the dew.

"Come on slowcoach, race yer up to that bush! Ready... steady... gaw!" She's already running. Trixie's there with her, yapping with excitement.

The mist clears quickly as the sun gets higher and the magical dew silently disappears as we walk the now familiar route. It suddenly feels very warm and we're walking much more slowly. . .

"Georgie. . .why do you think the new ones have been sent here?"

"I don't know. I've been wondering. I can't think why. . . they both seem sort of normal, especially Ayesha." I find myself going a bit dreamy when I say her name.

"Oooo Georgie! Could it be love?" Smidgin's looking right into my eyes in that funny challenging way that I'm getting used to. I change the subject, "So what do you think Lloyd's in for Smidgin?"

"I don't really know Georgie. I can't imagine him doin' anything wrong. P'raps he took his library books back late!"

Without thinking I say, "Ayesha must be in for being beautiful."

"Oooo Georgie, it *is* love isn't it!"

"I know Smidgin. Let's make up the reasons why they're here!"

"Yes! I've got a good one I've got a good one!"

"All right Smidg."

"Okay, ready? Ayesha, yeah? She's got into trouble spendin' too much money doin' internet shoppin'. . . and there aren't any computers here so she can't do it any more. And her parents are very rich so they'll pay off the money she owes and for her to come here!"

"Yup, like that one Smidg. I've got one for Lloyd now."

"Go Georgie!"

"Right, Lloyd's in even more trouble than Ayesha. He's been caught with binoculars at a military airport, spying for a small but powerful country called...what shall we call it...er... Mysteryland!"

"No – no – no - I've got it!" shouts Smidgin triumphantly, "Mysteriova!"

"Yeah- yeah- yeah! That's good Smidgin! High-five!"

Triumphant, we laugh so much we nearly cry.

***

I 'm getting very used to the breakfast banquet, (I think my days of grabbing a biscuit as I rush off to school are over), and I'm well pleased to smell the bacon as we get back to base. Getting our shoes off in the boot room, we wonder if Ayesha and Lloyd will be up yet.

"Have a nice walk yous two?" Maggie turns from the cooker, fish-slice in hand. "That dog's going to be sae fit; she'll miss you when you leave."

(Weird; the idea of leaving here doesn't seem so appealing now.)

"Yes thanks, it's always fun."

Ayesha and Lloyd are already sitting at the table, "Morning Ayesha!" I try to sound relaxed and cool but each time I look at her my heart comes up to my throat and my voice comes out choked.

"Good morning George, good morning Smidgin. Erm, please could I come on the next early morning walk. Will you wake me?"

"Course we will, won't we Georgie?" Smidgin turns to me and winks theatrically.

A little cough from the end of the table reminds us that Lloyd's there. He looks very sleepy under his unbrushed hair," Morning you two," he says in his deep muffled voice.

"Good morning Lloyd, you all right?" Smidgin and I speak at exactly the same time. We look at each other and we're laughing uncontrollably yet again.

"What are ye like yous two!" Maggie serves up our egg and bacon and puts the plates carefully on our placemats. We take a moment to say thank you, and gaze appreciatively at our food before we tuck in.

"Where's John, Maggie?"

"He's gone to Lochaire to meet your last wee pal. The boy was escorted on the train, but his carer had to go right back."

Everyone has stopped eating to listen to Maggie.

"What's he like Maggie? How old is he?" This is Smidgin, always to the point.

"We'ell. . . he's eleven years old, and ye'll have to ask him the rest for yourselves."

This news kind of unites us as a group and whilst we clear up the kitchen together the chat is all about what this boy might be like.

I'm just banging the dustpan into the bin when John gets back.

"Hey you guys! Meet Mikey!"

Mikey is black, small for eleven, with very close-cut hair and huge eyes. He's wearing street-style clothes, blue hip-hop jeans, a blue hoodie with a baseball motif and some very cool trainers.

He doesn't speak a word as we take it in turns to introduce ourselves, he just smiles a shy nervous little smile and his eyes widen even more as he shakes hands.

"Right you lot I'll be giving young Mikey his breakfast noo, whilst you all get on with your chores."

I'm on hoovering and Smidgin's on dusting. She's itching to talk about Mikey and shouts above the noise of the vacuum cleaner, "Can he talk do you think Georgie?"

"I should think so, why wouldn't he?"

"Well he hasn't said a word yet Georgie."

"He hasn't had much of a chance really, has he? And he's probably a bit overwhelmed by everything; remember how you felt when you first arrived."

"I wonder where he's from?"

"He looks like a city boy; the hip-hop look is definitely urban. He'll soon get used to us and then it'll be fun chatting with him and finding out all about him."

"What d'you think he's in for?"

"I don't know Smidgin. We'll find out sooner or later."

"Yeah, yeah Georgie. That makes three mysteries now."

***

At dinnertime we discover that Mikey actually doesn't speak. He nods for yes and shakes his head for no; he carries a notebook and pen in his jeans pocket to write down anything more complicated. But he can laugh out loud, a giggly chuckle which is so fun to hear, and he makes a normal sound when he coughs or sneezes. I'm thinking it probably isn't a physical problem that's stopping him speaking.

Another amazingly delicious meal is nearly at an end when John stands up and taps lightly on his cup with a spoon to get everyone's attention. This hasn't happened before and we all stop chatting straightaway.

"Well everyone, thank ye for your attention: firstly, whilst I've got the floor, I think we should take this opportunity to say a big thank you to Maggie for all the fantastic food she keeps preparing for us!"

We all turn to Maggie and clap enthusiastically. She bows and curtsies theatrically.

"Now," John continues," To business!"

This sounds interesting. I look round the table and see a different expression on each of the kid's faces; Ayesha looks intrigued, Lloyd looks a bit less sleepy than usual, and kind of surprised, Smidgin looks very serious as though she's worried about what the "business" might be, and poor little Mikey looks downright terrified.

"Don't all look sae worried. It'll be fun! Hard work as well but loads of fun nevertheless. Ye're all going as a group, well ye'll be a team in fact, to go on an unaccompanied one-night trek. Before I go on, I must reassure ye that your parents and carers are fully aware that ye're going to be doing this. They've all signed the consent forms so they must think ye're capable." He pauses and looks at each of us listening so intently; "Ye certainly look capable to me and we're going to teach you all the skills ye'll need, and more -  just in case. We start training in the morning. Now, any questions?"

So many questions, so much to take in; we all look blank. Eventually I ask, "How long are we going to be training and when will we go?"

"Right George," John answers, "Ye'll all be training for five days starting tomorrow. Ye'll be setting off on the sixth day. Other young people just like yourselves have achieved very well in that timescale."

Smidgin's finding it hard to stay on her seat; she's bouncing up and down with excitement; now she looks as though she will explode, "How are we goin' to go to bed if we're away for a night? Are we goin' to sleep on the ground under a tree?"

Maggie smiles gently and answers in a serious tone;

"Ye'll have tents to sleep in, one for the girls and one for the boys, and lovely warm sleeping bags."

"Oooo Maggie I've never been in a tent.  I 'ave been in a sleepin' bag though."

Smidgin's asking all the questions now, "What about food? I don't want to be hungry."

"And we most certainly don't want you to be hungry Smidgin," Maggie answers reassuringly "we're going to be packing your food into containers that'll have labels on to tell you when to use them, plus some extras of course. It'll all be fine and ye'll not be hungry."

"Where are we goin' to?"

"Good question Smidgin," John picks up a wooden spatula and points to various places on the *Ordnance Survey* map which is sellotaped to the kitchen door, "Look, we're here; the ruined croft is down here and the mountains are right here. And that's where ye're going. Not to do any mountain climbing mind! That would involve quite a lot more training and ye wouldn't be expected to do that unaccompanied!"

Smidgin has her hand in the air like at school, she's

waving now, obviously bursting to speak. John smiles broadly at her, "Yes Smidgin, what's your question?"

"Well it's a little bit embarrassin' really. . . what I want to know is. . .where will we go to the toilet?"

Everyone laughs, well, to be fair, only the kids, including Smidgin. Maggie speaks with due solemnity, "That's a very good and serious question Smidgin. For wees ye can all just find a bit of privacy behind a bush or tree or whatever; for poos ye have to dig a hole and very importantly, cover it up when ye've finished. There'll be a small spade in your equipment for that purpose. But we'll tell you exactly how to manage that as part of your training."

Smidgin struggles in vain to hide her giggles, "Yuck that's disgustin!" she manages to squeal.

Smidgin's giggles are highly infectious. I look at Ayesha and she's looking at me and we burst out laughing, then within seconds everyone around the table has caught it, even John and Maggie. It makes me feel liberated to be laughing at something so silly; it's like I'm released to be a little kid again. Eventually the giggles subside and John brings us back to order. He clears his throat.

"Ayesha, do ye have any camping experience?"

"A little bit, well a very little tiny bit actually. In my back garden we used to have sleepovers in a tent when I was much younger;" she blushes, "I suppose that doesn't really count does it?"

"Och aye lassie of course it does, it means ye've slept in a tent. That is camping experience."

Ayesha seems so relieved; she smiles and sighs deeply.

Now John turns to Lloyd. He speaks gently, "What about ye' young man, have ye' camped before?"

Lloyd looks up then down and makes some thoughtful faces; he's giving the question great consideration; we all lean towards him a bit when he begins to speak quietly and gruffly, "Yeah, well, when I was about eight I went to a sort of camping weekend with the cubs. But I, I, yeah I'm well up for an expedition."

He sounds faintly scared and maybe a bit embarrassed. At this point I begin to really like him.

John interjects promptly, I think to save Lloyd any more of that enormous effort, "Well that definitely qualifies as camping experience. And it's good to hear that ye're liking the idea of a wee bit of adventure. Now what about ye, George?"

I feel put on the spot a little bit because I don't want to sound like a know-it-all, "Er - I have done some camping and trekking. My mum and dad used to take me on camping holidays. I also did the Duke of Edinburgh Award. I had to do hikes for that."

"That's very good George, that's brilliant! Your experience will be fantastically helpful to yourself and all the team."

"So last but not least, young Mikey, have ye camped before?"

Mikey looks at all the other expectant faces around him before fully focussing on John, setting his mouth in a serious line, and shaking his head slowly and clearly.

"Well that's all right Mikey because you and Smidgin are going to have a whole lot of fun learning something completely new."

Smidgin just cannot resist this opportunity for a joke, "Yes! How to bury poo!"

Even Mikey cracks up at this; his smile and chuckle are like the sun breaking through clouds on a stormy day.

Now he leans back in his chair, pushes his legs out, and stretches his arms above his head, making him look the most relaxed I've seen since he arrived.

"Right, thank ye all for listening sae well - just one more wee thing; we start training in the morning. We've lots to do sae breakfast 'll be early, eight o'clock sharp. I'm going tae give ye each a wee alarm clock now, sae that ye can take responsibility for getting yourselves up and ready. I'll show ye how tae set them."

# TRAINING COMMENCES

The alarm clock may be little but it's loud! Too loud! Bang! It's off! I can't believe it actually is 7.30! The latest I've woken up since I've been here! There'll be no time for sleepy meandering thinking then. But whilst I get myself ready for the day, thoughts about all the kids crowd my head. Why doesn't Mikey speak? Why do Lloyd's thumbs keep moving all the time? And why does Ayesha sneak biscuits and bread from her plate up her sleeves when she thinks no-one's looking? At least I know the reasons for Smidgin being here, straightforward honest theft! And for her the holiday of a lifetime, the only holiday she's ever had.

All polished up, a squirt of Lynx Africa, and I'm ready for anything the day will bring.

About to open my door I stop still in the sudden realisation that I've got that positive optimistic feeling that I used to take for granted before my Dad's illness.

"Morning everyone," I'm the last to come to the table, and mostly they've got their mouths full and just nod and give a closed-mouth smile, except for Mikey who looks very worried – no - he looks more than worried - he looks scared. Why should he be frightened about a camping trip? When I was his age, I could hardly wait. I remember being impatient. Thinking about it now I was probably a bit of a pain!

I wonder whether I should try to help him feel happier about things by chatting and perhaps having a joke with him but as I look up from my food and see his closed expression I decide to give him more time to get used to being here.

When I'm about to bite into my third thickly buttered slice of toast, John stands up and tings on his cup with a spoon.

"Well everyone, it's very clear to me that ye're all enjoying your breakfast sae whatever ye do, don't stop on my account.  Just listen up whilst ye carry on with that serious eating. We're very lucky with the weather again this morning sae as soon as ye've cleared up after breakfast we're going outside to start training for the expedition. The first skill ye're going to learn is how to put up the tents.

*** 

I'm buzzing as Lloyd and I carry the tents outside on to the flat grass at the back of the building, "Lloyd, what d'you think? Are you looking forward to this?"

"Well, to be honest, I don't know if I'll be any good at it. I don't want to look like an idiot in front of everyone."

"It'll be all right Lloyd, they'll show us what to do - that's the point of training; to give us all the skills we need."

"Oh yeah, see what you mean - just need to concentrate I suppose."

John and Maggie are sitting on the grass making a fuss of Trixie as we go across to them. They both shade their eyes to look up to us because we have our backs to the sun. "All set and ready to learn then ye' two?" John smiles," Ah here come the others, now we can get cracking. George, take your tent over to Maggie and team up with Ayesha, Lloyd stay with me and Mikey and Smidgin."

Can't believe my luck, me and Ayesha together, a dream ticket!

I do know how to put this particular tent up so although I find it hard to take in what Maggie's saying as she demonstrates the method, I know I'll be fine with it. She's very good. It takes her ten minutes tops! She has definitely done this a few times before.

"Now yous two I'm going to take it down and pack it away, then ye can have a go for yourselves."

I watch the packing very carefully; I want to get it exactly right and I know that packing these tents away is the most difficult thing. Ayesha's watching very carefully as well; I think to myself that she's probably very competitive and she'll almost certainly be better at this than me.

Maggie finishes the process with a triumphant pulling of the drawstrings on the immaculately packed tent-bag. She pats it and presents it to me.

"Your turn!"

I open the drawstrings and empty the bag on to the grass. As I start to shake it out Ayesha's on it like a whirlwind, shaking it, smoothing it out, locating the right rods for the right channels; I feel a little bit helpless and hopeless watching this superfast performance. . . I stand, frozen, in awe. . .

"Come on then George, give us a hand!"

She's got to the bit where it's much easier with two people,  where you have to feed the bendy poles through the channels. I know it can be tricky getting the poles past the seams so I kind of hope that she'll have a problem with it. Then I can sort it out and look cool and experienced. No such luck, she gives the impression that she's done this hundreds of times before.

"Okay George, let's put the pegs in now."

I pick up the peg- bag and open it up as quickly as I can. I pass her half of the pegs, then I go to the other side of the tent and start releasing the guy ropes ready to fasten down. I want to win at this at least . . . shame on me. . . I somehow fumble a rope and it gets tangled, so I have to sort it out and, by the time I've done that, she's holding her hand out for more pegs because she's finished all hers!

Now she stands back to admire, (yes...let's face it), her handiwork. Maggie carefully checks all around the tent.

"I canna believe ye've no done this before Ayesha, pretty impressive ay George?"

"Yup," I nod, mock-reluctantly, "She's good. Well done Ayesha!"

"Okay time to pack away again you two," Maggie watches our efforts for a while and then goes across the grass to see how the other group's getting on.

"Ayesha are you sure you haven't put a tent up before?" I ask, just to start a conversation.

"No honestly, I just always concentrate when I'm being taught something because I really hate getting things wrong. In fact, I'm a bit crazy like that. It's to do with. . ."

She tails off like I do when I realise that I'm about to give away more than I'm comfortable with. Sighing deeply, she looks away into the distance.

"Enough talking George," she changes tack with a jokily posh strict voice, "We have work to do!"

Now I take the lead because I feel confident that you need to have practised this to do it well and I reckon I can score some clever points.

More fool me. Somehow, instead of a neatly folded tent with the pegs tucked in the middle, I end up with an untidy mess three times the size of the bag it's got to fit into.

Better than clever points, it makes her laugh and laugh. . . rippling peals of silver chimes. "Oh George!" the silver bells stop ringing, "That is completely hopeless! Come here."

I put the green bag with the tent fountaining out of it into Ayesha's welcoming arms.

"Right young George," she says in a schoolteacher voice, "Concentrate this time!"

"Yes miss," I say in a tiny voice, hoping to hear that laugh again, but no such luck, she pulls out the sad mess that I've made of the tent and places it on the grass. Now I assist in a masterclass of tent folding.

"Gotta hand it to you Ayesha, it looks like you are tentmaster supreme! You are going to have to be in overall charge of the tents on the expedition."

"And you George, are a master of verbal waffle and you're not going to get out of all the work that easily."

I'm trying to think of a witty reply when I find Smidgin, Trixie at her heels, pulling my elbow excitedly, "Georgie, Georgie, we did it! We put up our own tent. It's great Georgie, it's lovely inside, everything looks green because it's a green tent. After lunch we've got to do it again so that when we go away, we can do it dead quick."

As usual when Smidgin's around I find I'm smiling, "Did you enjoy that then Smidgin, are you good at it?"

"Yeah, dead good. John says we make a really good team!"

***

Lunch is the loudest meal yet. There's loads of excited chatter and everyone seems to be shining from being in the air all morning. Even Mikey looks happy as he "talks" energetically with Smidgin. Every now and then they both rock with laughter.

I'm sitting between Lloyd and Ayesha. I think we all feel quite cool, kind of grown-up really, as we watch the smaller ones enjoying themselves.

"How did you get on with tent-pitching Lloyd?" I ask him, suddenly remembering his worries this morning.

"Well er – yeah - it was kind of all right really. There's a sort of system to it, a kind of well, strategy really, and I'm good at strategies."

"Well done mate." Do I sound a bit patronising?

Maybe not, he's absolutely beaming with pleasure at that morsel of praise.

"So, this afternoon we have to put the tents up then take them down again just one more time and then that's covered," Ayesha sums up in her matter-of-fact can-do way.

"What about packing them away then?" I can't help saying it, and I get my reward. . . that amazing laugh.

"Er, am I missing something?" Lloyd asks ponderously.

"No not really Lloyd," Ayesha manages to speak calmly, "It's just that tent packing wasn't George's strong point and I think he should be the one to pack away this afternoon because he is the one who definitely needs practice."

"Right everybody," John calls us to order, "Ye've all worked very hard today, just one more practice on pitching and putting away and those skills will be in your pockets. When ye've done that we'll all go on a wee walk to commence your physical training."

We clear the lunch up quickly. We're all looking forward to testing our skills one more time.

"What do you think Ayesha?"

She has timed me with a stopwatch, but although I was working for speed, she still checks each part of the tent carefully to make sure it's done perfectly.

"It'll pass I suppose George," she answers, "but I won't look too carefully at it!"

My packing away is better this time, I get all of the tent into the bag anyway. She laughs, "Maybe that will have to be my job after all."      "It would just be rude to argue with you about that Ayesha," I say with some relief.

"Or maybe you should spend some more time practising!"

Like the gentleman I am I don't push my luck and I let her have the last word.

# AYESHA EXPLAINS

I watch Ayesha at afternoon break which we have outside on the grass. There's tea and amazing home-made buttery crumbly shortbread triangles. She drinks her tea in tiny sips and nibbles delicately at her shortbread, as though it might bite her, and then, after looking to see if anyone is aware, she surreptitiously passes it to Trixie who gulps it down in one.

Seeing this makes my spine tingle because it reminds me of the dream I had at the croft in which the little girl fed the dog under the table, and also because I suddenly realise that Ayesha's behaviour could be a major clue to the reason she's at Summerlands.

Maggie comes over with the tray of shortbread, "Any more for any more?"

I can't resist. Why should I even try? "Thank you, Maggie, that is the best!"

"What about you Ayesha?" Maggie asks.

"Thank you, Maggie, it really is delicious, but I am totally full up," Ayesha's making a full-up face and patting her tummy convincingly.

I am not convinced.

\*\*\*

John takes the lead on this training hike; he says we need to walk for at least two hours a day to get us "expedition-fit". Lloyd walks alongside him, Smidgin and

Mikey are in the middle of the crocodile, and Ayesha and I take up the rear.

 Everyone ahead of us is chatting away and Ayesha and I are no different.

"Do you like it here George?"

"Yes, yes, I hate to admit it Ayesha, but for me it gets better every day."

"Where are you from?"

"North London, Tottenham, do you know it?"

"I'm from Surrey. It's very near London. Of course, I've heard of it, my dad goes to a hospital there sometimes."

Oh no... I wasn't expecting this... has she got a sick dad? What can I say to her? What did people say to me? I say the only thing I can say, "I'm really sorry, how long has he been ill?"

"He's not ill George, he's fine but he does visit a lot of hospitals. He's a doctor, a consultant oncologist, that means a . . ."

"Yeah, Yeah, I know what that means . . .a cancer specialist." I almost hug her in relief, I wouldn't want her to have to go through what mum and I did.

We walk on in silence for a bit then we both start talking at the same time,

"No, you first," she says in her perfectly polite way.

"I was going to ask you about the rest of your family,

brothers and sisters, and your mum, that sort of thing."

"You'll regret asking that one. Once I start talking about them, I never stop!"

"But I do actually want to know Ayesha. And we've got loads of time."

"Alright then. Don't say I didn't warn you! You know about my dad already, so I'll start with my mum." Ayesha pushes a few little tendrils of hair away from her shining brown eyes and speaks with passion.    "Mum's wonderful, I know most mums are to their children, but she's been so strong for me . . ." She trails off, wipes her eyes softly then clears her throat. "Mum's a nurse. That's how she met my dad. She only works part-time at the moment because she likes to be able to be there when any of us need her. I've got two younger sisters.  Saida's twelve and very brainy, she loves science and animals and wants to be a vet. She's really great, so enthusiastic about everything. My other sister's called Zubeida, she's ten; I think she's probably a genius! She's great at art, you know, drawing and painting and modelling with clay. She's the quiet one, so beautiful, so loving. I love them all so much . . . it was their love that pulled me through . . . We've got a cat as well, she's called Squash, she's a fantastic tabby, oh - I feel a bit homesick thinking about her. It's your turn now George, tell me all about you."

I want to ask her what the problem was that her family got her through but now doesn't feel the right time. I figure I probably know already anyway.

I take a deep breath, "I have the best mum in the

world as well."

"No!" Ayesha laughs, "Mine's the best!" She looks at me and I force a smile.

"But I lost my dad at the end of last year. He died of cancer."

"Oh George . . ."

Now there's one of those cavernous silences that I've got so used to.

We come to a halt and stand facing each other.

"It's all right Ayesha, you don't have to say anything. I know people feel sad for me when I tell them; I don't think there's anything anyone can say. I got really angry, so angry that in the end I even threw a chair at a teacher. I got kicked out of school. I've been sent here to help me deal with it. And it seems to be working already. For a start it's good just to be somewhere so different. And it's strange but I'm finding that it's good to have some time without my mum. She's gone to see her sister in Australia"

"Yup George, I think Summerlands is working some magic on me as well. I'm here to help me with my recovery from anorexia." She looks searchingly to gauge my reaction. I nod my head slowly in encouragement... like my counsellor would... "I had the best life, and I knew it, an amazing family, my own room in a lovely house, good friends, music lessons. I love playing the cello.

I started to feel pressure when school said I should take my GCSEs a year early. It wasn't their fault though. I pressured myself because that's what I'm like. Studying the whole time and hardly sleeping at night. And that's when it began. Everything was as good as it could be in my life until this horrible disease got into my head and kept telling me that I was rubbish in every way. It told me to starve myself because the thinner I got the better things would be for me. I nearly died of starvation. I had to be pushed in a wheelchair and my hair started to fall out. I was totally unaware of how ill I was. I feel so guilty George, because of what I put my family through. And I was totally unaware of their suffering at the time."

She's looking kind of pleadingly at me as if asking for my forgiveness.

I'm stunned; I want to say something that will make her feel better, but I'm scared of saying the wrong thing. I expect she's as used to these more- than- awkward silences as me.

I say nothing. I just look into her eyes and take her cool soft hand and squeeze it gently; I give it a little rub then put it back at her side. I think she knows that I will do my best to help whenever she needs me.

The others have stopped some way ahead. They're all shouting at the tops of their voices for us to catch up. Ayesha turns to me smiling massively. "Beat you there George!

# FINDING OUT ABOUT LLOYD

I go along to breakfast a bit early figuring that I can get a head start in the cuppa stakes, but as I get near to the closed kitchen door, I hear what sounds like a very emotional conversation going on.

Although their voices aren't raised, I hear Maggie, John and Lloyd. And Lloyd sounds upset.

"I only need my iphone for five flipping minutes! I need to check what's going on in the zone!" He's speaking much more clearly and forcefully than I've heard him speak before. This must mean a lot to him.

John answers in a calm but very firm tone, "Lloyd, we understand that this cold- turkey treatment is really hard for ye'. . . but we know it works. Ye've come a long way already, ye've done sae well. Tae give in now would take ye right back to square one in your recovery. Ye know that. Ye're an intelligent young man.

At this point I realise to my horror that I have been eavesdropping on a very private conversation and I creep back quickly to my room. I know immediately that I mustn't tell anyone what I heard, however tempting it might be.

*\*\**

When I go to try again for a cuppa the kitchen door is open. To my surprise I see Lloyd standing by the cooker frying a pancake.

"Good morning to ye George! Did ye sleep well?" Maggie is cheery and welcoming as always, "We discovered that Lloyd's favourite food is pancakes, so we thought we might as well make enough for everyone. . . do you like them George?"

"I love pancakes. What a brilliant idea!"

I'm thinking to myself that this is just what mum would do when I was little to get me out of a bad mood. She would distract me, very often with some cooking.

Lloyd turns from the cooker as he shuffles the pan, looking more animated and happier than I've seen him before, "Watch this George!" he flips the pancake perfectly.

"That's fantastic Lloyd! Well done! Is it for me?"

Lloyd turns to Maggie, "Is that - er -  okay Maggie?"

"Yes of course Lloyd, just keep them coming!"

What is it about pancakes that gives you an appetite when you maybe weren't even thinking about food before? I've devoured four of Lloyd's delicious creations smothered in maple syrup and squirty cream before even looking up. He's looking expectantly at me, frying pan in hand complete with light golden pancake number five when I'm saved from my greed by Smidgin.

"Wowee pancakes! My absolutely top favourite! George, are you 'avin' that one?"

"No thanks Smidgin, if it's all right with Lloyd that fantastic pancake is definitely yours!" I look at Lloyd who is smiling widely at all this positive feedback and he carefully slides the pancake on to Smidgin's plate.

"What would you like with it Smidgin? We have lemon and sugar, strawberry jam, golden syrup, maple syrup, squirty cream . . ."

This is the most I've heard Lloyd speak in one go and I'm so astonished that I feel my mouth drop open. Smidgin doesn't seem to notice though as she solemnly ponders her choices, "Well chef, I think I will 'ave to start off with strawberry jam on me first one and then work me way through the other toppings with each of me pancakes."

Lloyd passes her the jam and then triumphantly makes his way back to the cooker, looking thrilled at the prospect of being kept on this possibly never- ending task.

As I thought, pancakes are a no-brainer. Everybody loves them, even Ayesha who eats a whole one with, I notice happily, maple syrup and a little bit of squirty cream, yeah!

Looks like another example of Summerland magic.

Having cooked for everyone, including John and Maggie, the chef is enjoying his own breakfast when John calls us to attention, "First of all everyone, please show your appreciation for our new chef!"

We all turn our pancake-happy faces to Lloyd who is eating contentedly with a certain amount of cream around his beaming smile.

"Three cheers for Lloyd!" I hear myself shout almost to my own surprise.

Cheers wholeheartedly given, John takes the floor

again, "Today, ladies and gentlemen, we will be continuing our physical training with another nice long hike."

He waits with a patient smile for the obligatory low-level protest groans to subside, "But first of all, whilst we're still all seated your wee team has to choose a leader."

I feel a bit challenged by John's announcement. I quickly realise that it's because if there has to be a leader, which of course I know there does when I think about it, I want it to be me. My wobbly moment passes when I look round the table and see all my friends looking at me.

"Now," continues John, "There are two different ways we can do this. We can either give you each a piece of paper and you can write down the name of the person you would like to be in overall charge on your expedition, which would be a secret ballot. Or you can just do a show of hands."

"Have a wee think aboot it for a minute."

Everyone looks very thoughtful; I'm wondering if I should choose Lloyd or Ayesha.

"Okay," John says, after a couple of minutes during which all that can be heard is the ever-present ticking of the big kitchen clock, "First of all raise your hand if ye would like a secret vote, where ye write the name down."

Only Mikey puts up his hand and then after looking around worriedly he quickly puts it down again.

John addresses Mikey quietly and kindly, "Mikey it'll be fine for you to write your vote down if you want to."

Mikey looks relieved. He nods.

Maggie tears a page from the kitchen notepad and passes it to Mikey. He holds up his own pen.

John stands up, "Right everyone, this is what we'll do. Each person has one vote which you can use to vote for anyone in the team - except yourself." We all laugh, breaking the slight tension that has built up.

"Ye must all remember that ye will have to trust the leader you vote for tae   listen tae ye, but that she or he will have the final say in any decisions concerning the expedition. Do ye all understand? Any questions"

Everybody looks very solemn except Smidgin who's bouncing up and down on her seat and nodding and smiling a huge meaningful smile right at me.

"Okay team! It's time to vote. Mikey you can write down your choice now and I will announce each person's name in the order that they arrived at Summerlands." He clears his throat.

"The first option is George."

At this, all of my friends, even Lloyd, cheer, bang on the table, then wave both hands in the air. Mikey holds his voting slip up; there is my name in big clear capitals.

"Congratulations George! You are quite obviously the candidate of choice. Would ye like to address any words to your team?"

I feel myself blushing and tears coming to my eyes. I stand up and say the first words that come into my head.

They sound strangely like the cub promise that I learnt when I was seven! "I promise that I will do my very best to keep you all safe. Thank you for choosing me. . .now please can I have a cup of tea!"

They are all laughing and clapping as Maggie passes me a monster cuppa.

\*\*\*

We're sitting on the huge squashy red sofas in the common room because it's lashing down with rain and, in Maggie's words, "Blowing a hoolie" outside.  Trixie's practically on Smidgin's lap, being lovingly stroked and whispered to. I'm watching them and thinking that this complete turnaround in the relationship between those two must be a miracle or perhaps is just another little bit of Summerlands magic, when John and Maggie come into the room.  They sit themselves down, side by side, on the one empty sofa. Maggie clears her throat in that "I have an announcement" kind of way and we all turn our heads, ready to listen.

"Today team, we're going to learn some basic first-aid. We always teach this near the end of the training week because people learn better when they've got used to being here and so they're more relaxed. Also, because what ye learn will be fresher in your heads when ye're off on the trek!

Has anyone done any first-aid training before?"

Ayesha puts her hand up a fraction after me. Nobody else does.

"Right, you two," Maggie continues," I wonder whose training is the most recent?"

I look at Ayesha. She looks kind of apologetic as she speaks, "I did an advanced course a few weeks ago, just before I came here. To fill in some time really. It seemed like a good idea," she trails off.

"Och Ayesha don't be embarrassed!" Maggie's delighted, "That's fantastic news. I suspect your training isn't quite as recent as that George?" She raises her eyebrows questioningly at me.

"No, no, nothing like as recent, it was two years ago, and it was just basic level for my D of E camping expedition."

"Right then. Ayesha, that would seem to settle it. Would ye like to be the official team first-aider?"

Now it's Ayesha's turn to be pleased to bits and very emotional and embarrassed at the same time.

"Yes, yes, of course I would, thank you!"

"That's really good. Well done Ayesha! Ye'll be carrying the first aid kit then. Okay team! It's fantastic that ye have a well- qualified first -aider going with ye but it's still very important for all of you to listen up and learn all ye can this morning."

"Yes!" pipes up Smidgin, "Because who will look after Ayesha if she gets hurt?"  We all laugh, Smidgin has, as usual," hit the nail right on the head," as my dad would say.

## THE ADVENTURE BEGINS

I wake up with my refreshed first-aid knowledge buzzing round my head. My new status as team-leader has made me painfully conscious of my responsibility to take on board anything and everything that will help keep my crew safe. I had concentrated really hard... "recovery position...arterial bleed...choking... unconsciousness... fractures...sprains..."

I lie in bed bringing up each condition in my head and then testing myself to see if I can remember the right responses. I think I'm pretty much okay. But it's very good to know that we'll have an ace first-aider with us - plus she'll be carrying a manual.

"Georgie, George, are you awake yet, Georgie, George, it's today! it's today! Can I come in Georgie boy? I've brought yer tea!" Her sing-song voice and wonderful hopefulness make me smile as always.

"Come in Smidgin, good morning." I say, looking at my clock which says five

thirty and thinking to myself that in most normal peoples' minds it's still night.

"Thanks for the tea Smidgin, I really appreciate it."

I really do appreciate this syrupy sickly beverage because I know how much love she puts in along with the sugar.

"Guess what Georgie?" She doesn't wait for me to reply. "They've put the rucksacks out in the common room.

One for each of us, with our names on, oooh, yours looks pretty big Georgie!"

"Oh no!" I give the appropriate worried reaction. "Smidgin, thanks for the tea. Please could you take my cup to the kitchen. I'll get dressed and see you in the common room in five minutes."

It feels like Christmas. I'm almost shaking with excitement as I hurriedly throw on the hiking clothes we were given last evening. They're like army kit -loose-fitting trousers, shirt, jacket and floppy hat all in a shade of light muddy green.

Catching a glimpse in the mirror as I rush out of the door, I wonder who it is for a second. The person in the mirror looks so motivated and practically shining with happiness.

Smidgin has tipped the contents of her own rucksack out on to the floor.

"Look George, isn't it excitin'?"

"It's a brilliant surprise Smidgin." They didn't tell us they were going to do this. "It's fantastic but it's still very early so we'll try to keep our voices down a bit, so as not to wake the others. Right, let's pack your stuff away and we can see what you've got at the same time."

Smidgin finds it almost impossible to keep her "Oooohs" And "Aaaahs" down as we line up her equipment on the floor. Everything's new and shiny; from sleeping bag, to torch, to bowl, plate and cutlery. I suddenly remember feeling made up just like her as when I went shopping with

Mum and Dad for our first camping trip...

I must have looked a bit serious for a moment, and, as always, Smidgin's notices.

"Georgie, what's the matter?"

"Nothing, Smidgin, happy memories that's all. Now we're making new happy memories. Come on, we need to pack this back in very neatly or it won't fit."

I'm smiling now, thinking of my fiasco with folding the tent, and Ayesha.

"Good morning Smidgin, morning George." It's Ayesha; she must've crept in very quietly, "What are you two up to so early in the morning?"

"Oooooh look Ayesha, we've all got all this brand-new stuff for our campin' trip," Smidgin is practically bursting with excitement as she spreads her good news.

Ayesha immediately tunes in to her mood, "Wow Smidgin that's fantastic! When you've finished putting your things away, we can tip mine out and see what I've got."

Smidgin's quick to respond, "Ooooh goody Ayesha! You might have some different stuff to me. Ahm just so excited ahm ready to burst!"

With Ayesha in charge, Smidgin's re-packing is soon done and it's almost certainly even neater than it originally was.

I'm watching the two girls and thinking how amazing it is how they are getting on so well together.  Nobody would have a clue that they've only known each other for ten days. Then a sudden handclap just behind my ear makes me jump out of my wits. "Mikey!"

He gives me a little push on the back and then runs off. I give chase. He's very fast out of the door and off over the moor. At least Trixie can keep up with him. I'm left well behind. I can't believe how fast he is.

I keep chasing. He must've covered 800 metres at the same speed! I reckon it must have become a bit real and a bit scary to him, like when my dad used to chase me. Although I knew it was totally for fun a tiny sharp element of fear would always come in. I'm catching him up now... I'm going to rugby tackle him...

"Gotcha!"

He lands on a fat clump of heather with a thud and bursts out laughing. I haven't heard him making this much noise before. It's amazing.

"Come on Mikey let's get back; we need to save our energy for the hike."

As I take his hands to pull him up, he stops laughing and looks stricken.

"Come on mate it's going to be fun. We'll all look after you... don't worry."

He looks searchingly into my eyes. I know he's trying to work out how he can convince me of the enormity of his fear.

"Mikey, seriously, I know you're frightened, but I

don't know what of. Can you tell me? I won't tell anyone else if you don't want me to."

He looks at me sadly and solemnly. He bows his head. Huge tears course down his cheeks.

"We need talk to John and Maggie about this Mikey. It's their job to look after all of us. They wouldn't want you to be scared and upset."

He looks even more scared as he grips my wrists strongly and shakes his head violently.

Silently I resolve to talk to them.

We walk slowly back to the house. Mikey goes in first, head and shoulders drooping with Trixie following steadfastly at his heels.

***

"Hey Georgie boy! Wha's wrong? You look like you lost a pound and found a penny! We're goin' on our big adventure today...remember?"

"You're absolutely right as usual Smidgin. There is a problem, but I hope I can sort it out before we leave. I have to try anyway."

"I'm going to talk to John and Maggie. I think they'll be able to help."

"Okay Georgie, see you in a bit."

She must have known how worried I felt because normally she would definitely have pestered me to tell her what was up.

*** 

Maggie and John'll be getting the breakfast ready in the kitchen. I shouldn't think there'll be anybody else in there. The door is slightly ajar. I hear happy chatter.  I take a deep breath and knock.

"Hello, come in," John calls, "George, Good morning! What can we do for ye?'"

"Is it okay if I close the door?  It's kind of tricky"

"Sure George", John sounds concerned, "Come and sit down. Cup of tea? There's some in the pot."

"Yes please, that'd be great."  We sit in a triangle, me John and Maggie, like on my first night here.

"Reet now my laddie," John's tone is gentle and reassuring, "What's the problem?"

"It's not about me, it's about Mikey. Is it okay if I talk to you about him? Only I'm really worried." Both Maggie and John nod their encouragement.

"He's terrified about going on the hike. I've been trying to reassure him that everything will be alright - that we'll look after him - but he's just not convinced. I asked him what he's scared of and that made him even worse. There's no way I'm ever going to get an answer from him. I'm worried that he'll be too nervous to enjoy it. It's going to make it really hard for him..."  I trail off in a hopeless helpless kind of way.

I take a big sip of tea and then sit back looking at my hands. The silence is broken only by the ticking of the clock for what seems like ages.

At last Maggie speaks, "George, your friends have chosen a good leader. Ye've just proved them right by coming right to us with your concerns. The fact is George that we canna tell ye anything about any other young person here because of a strict confidentiality policy. That's not to say ye were wrong to ask us, not at all, far from it. It proves tae us what we already knew, that ye're a mature and caring young man."

John takes over now, "My advice would be tae make him feel as safe and secure as ye can. He may well open up tae ye' at some point, and that would be a good thing for him as well as ye."

I can't think of an answer to what they've told me. Basically they've told me nothing about Mikey. But they have told me something about me. That they trust me to look after Mikey. I thank them and go back to my team.

***

They cheer as I walk in the door. Smidgin comes and hugs me, "Where've you been Georgie? We thought you'd deserted us."

"John and Maggie wanted to give me some last-minute instructions." Not even a fib really, I inwardly pat myself on the back for quick thinking. I'm beginning to feel like a real leader now - or perhaps the head of the family.

"Right now everybody, have you all checked your

rucksacks and packed everything back in? Can you look all around to make sure nothing's left out?" I clearly remember doing this with my mum and dad. We would always find something really important that we'd left out at this point, like a can-opener or a torch.

We all bustle around the common room checking under sofas, cushions and any other clutter.

"Have you all got everything then?" Everyone replies at the same time with a loud "Yes George!"  And of course, this makes Smidgin giggle, so within seconds we're all giggling.  I feel so much better after that laugh it's amazing. Now I'm ready to continue with the preparations.

"Lloyd you're the navigator; have you got the map and compass?"

"Er...I think so...just double-checking."

"Ayesha, you're first-aider, have you got the first-aid kit and manual?"

"Aye aye sir!" She stands to attention and salutes; everybody laughs.

"Smidgin, you are chief carer of Trixie, have you got her bowl and food?"

Smidgin is laughing so much she can hardly speak... but following Ayesha's lead she does eventually manage to salute and shout out, "Aye aye sir!"

"Right Mikey, you are in charge of pens and writing paper; have you got them?"

He seems to have calmed down as he gives a little nod and smile and pats his securely fastened rucksack.

"Well done Mikey, well done everybody. It looks like we're ready to go. Let's put these in the boot room and go and get breakfast."

*** 

Breakfast is a massive affair. More eating, more drinking and more and louder exuberant chatter than usual. I guess everyone's stoking up for the trip, (and maybe just a bit excited!).

As soon as John tings the glass for attention the noise stops. We know that this will be our final instructions before we begin our epic adventure.

"All right folks thank you for listening. I have only three things to tell you; the first is that Maggie and I are sure you are all ready and able to complete this trip successfully. The second is that you have chosen your own leader and you must trust him to make final decisions on any issues that may arise. Finally, and very importantly, remember to have fun! Over to you George."

"Thank you John and Maggie for all the work you've put into this. A round of applause for John and Maggie everybody and then we're outta here!"

There's even more noise now. John and Maggie stand at the kitchen doorway and shake each person's hand as we go through.

***

We're all dressed exactly the same; apart from our hats that is. We're wearing army-style camouflage suits, they're loose and comfortable, ideal for hiking, and it's fun all being dressed the same. It makes us feel even more of a team. For a bit of individuality, we each have our own choice of hat. Mikey and Smidgin are both wearing red baseball caps. They look a proper pair.

Ayesha's hat is a bluey-green camping-type floppy. Her face seems to be alight under it, her teeth flashing perfect white as she talks animatedly with Lloyd who, for the first time that I've seen, actually does look excited.

Lloyd and I have chosen to wear the army-type bush hats that came with the camouflage suits.  It all feels like a big kid's game.  I get a sudden surge of happy excitement like a kind of arrow through my stomach. My worries and doubts about looking after the team vanish. I feel one hundred per cent sure that whatever happens we'll all be fine in the end.

I have to say it, well it's traditional isn't it, "Does anyone need the toilet before we set off?"

One by one they each decide that's a good idea. And when they've all gone, I think I might as well go too.

Now it's time to get walking boots and rucksacks on. I check that everyone is comfortable, which was something I learnt to do on my D of E training.

"Okay Team, let's get outta here!"

As navigator Lloyd takes the lead. Ayesha's walking next to him. Mikey and Smidgin walk side by side behind them and I take up the rear. At the moment this is the best place for me. I can see how everybody's coping with the pace and also spot anything they might drop, such as a water bottle from a rucksack side-pocket, which of course I soon find myself picking up!

It's a fantastic day. Although the sun's shining there's this cool breeze sending little fluffy white clouds shooting across the bright blue sky. Ideal walking weather.  What a brilliant start!

So why do I feel this faint nagging sense of unease, this feeling of a dark shadow hanging over me... over the whole group... but mostly over Mikey?  How could anyone or anything be near enough to threaten us? It's obvious that Mikey doesn't feel safe; he's shown that by the way he jumps out of his skin when there's a loud or unusual noise and the way he looks carefully into a room before entering. He has shown it by his massive reluctance to coming on this trip. Maybe I'm just in sympathy with his feelings...maybe that's not a bad thing though.

I catch up with Lloyd and Ayesha, "How's it going so far you two?"

Ayesha answers enthusiastically, "I am absolutely loving it George. I feel the best I have for as long as I can remember. I'm nearly bursting with it. I feel so free!"

Lloyd's not quite so full of joy, "Yeah George man, this is okay, I'm feeling okay."

Smidgin and Mikey are marching on and still finding plenty to talk about; they look fine, but I'll check anyway. I get in stride with them.

"Alright Mikey? Alright Smidgin?"

They're so engrossed in their conversation that I make them jump. A flash of fear crosses Mikey's face but then he smiles at me and nods.

Smidgin, as usual, has something to say, "Georgie boy it's great innit? This trip is so excitin' I'm goin' to remember it me whole life and I'm going to come back and bring me mum and if I have kids, I'll bring them here too, I love it so much!"

"And how are you Trixie?" She has come trotting back to us, tongue hanging out and panting, "Ahh you're thirsty Trix!" I bend down and smooth her head.

"I think we'll stop for a break now - everyone agree?"

The answer is immediate and clear. Everybody drops to the ground as one. Trixie gets her drink first. Smidgin lies on her tummy on the ground with her face near to the water bowl. When Trixie starts lapping up the water noisily and messily Smidgin gets splashed, "Oo Trixie what are you doin'? I didn't ask you to wash me face!" Making spluttering noises she collapses into uncontrollable giggles. Those giggles are contagious and in seconds we're all laughing...

"Right, snack anyone?"

I chuck out a chocolate biscuit to each of the crew and we all have a drink from our water bottles. When I stand up to check for any loose litter, I think I see the movement of a human figure far back from where we have walked. I rub my eyes and strain them to confirm what I thought I saw. We are far from the croft so it wouldn't be those ghosts. Would it? Maybe it was a cow or a sheep...but I can't see anything...if there was anything it has totally disappeared.

I take off my hat, scratch my head and stretch my arms up as high as I can to try to dispel my strange unease. Maybe it's just tiredness.

"You alright George?" Ayesha sounds concerned, she's looking questioningly into my eyes and it's not just a throwaway comment. I wonder for a moment whether I should tell her about my niggling worry but I decide to just wait and see because it probably is nothing, I could easily be imagining things. I take a massive deep breath, "Yup Ayesha, it's all going okay so far, I think. Are you okay?" She nods and smiles, "Yes thanks George, very okay."

Looking back again I see nothing but low scrub, and trees and heather. Time to move on then. "Hope you've had enough rest guys, because we have to get marching again!"

"Aaw Georgie boy do we 'ave to?"

I know Smidgin's saying it for fun but I answer her solemnly, "If you want to sleep in a tent tonight we have to get a move on so that we can put it up whilst it's still light."

She springs to her feet, stands to attention and salutes, "Aye aye captain, yes sir!"

Although it's getting hotter quickly, so hot that there

are mirages, we are still walking at a good steady pace. That break really helped. I realise that I wouldn't even have thought about stopping if it hadn't been for Trixie needing a drink, and I make a mental note to stop every hour or maybe more often than that whilst it's so hot.

I stay at the back of the line. I feel like I have become the rear guard now. I need to protect my team. Every now and then I turn around to see if anything or anyone's there. Sometimes, out of the corner of my eye, I actually think I see a figure, or even two, but as quickly as I catch sight of them, they're gone. Maybe because of this new and massive responsibility I've become a bit paranoid! Maybe, I think wildly, I've got a touch of sunstroke. I decide to try to not look so often.

"Owww!" I'm brought back from my deep worried thoughts by a scream.

"Oh Smidgin what happened?"

She's sitting on a mound of heather rubbing her ankle with a pained expression on her face.

"I fell down a hole. I think it was a rabbit hole, like Alice in Wonderland!"

This thought seems to cheer her up, "I've never been anywhere near a rabbit hole before, it's dead good isn't it?"

She's forgotten her pain but I'm anxious to see how bad the damage is.

Ayesha's already crouching down to examine the injury,

"If I just hold your heel up a bit Smidgin do you think you could try and wiggle your foot very gently?"

"Owww, that hurts a bit"

"Just a bit Smidgin? Or a lot? Is it a sharp pain or a dull pain?"

"It's not sharp, it's more like being hit with a stick than poked with a stick."

"I think it's a bruise, maybe a sprain. I'll put a stretchy bandage on it. We'll have to support you while you walk." She shouts out to everyone, "When we get going can everyone look out for a walking stick for Smidgin please!"

Ayesha's so good at this. She's like a really good nurse or doctor who makes you feel better just by being there.

Mikey's been watching. He's concerned for Smidgin but he's also very agitated by the break in our progress. He's continually looking all around us and frowning, rubbing his hands and jumping from one foot to the other. I can see he'll feel better when we get moving again.

"Smidgin come and hold on to my arm!"

"Lloyd, could you go the other side please."

Smidgin's giggling gleefully as she hooks her arms round ours, "This is turning out to be even more fun than I thought...ouch!"

"You alright Smidgin?" Lloyd sounds properly concerned.

"That did 'urt a bit Lloyd, but 'ow could I not be alright with two such 'andsome young men 'elping me along?"

Trixie bounces and yaps at our heels with excitement at this new spectacle of Smidgin limping along between me and Lloyd.

Without the distraction of Smidgin's jokes and antics Mikey's still casting frequent anxious looks around him. Ayesha's quick to spot the problem and goes to walk by his side. He looks up at her face as she chats and some of his tension seems to ease.

## AN UNPLANNED DELAY

Progress is getting slower now, what with the casualty, and the heat of the sun increasing by the second. Everyone, including me, is struggling. I glance at my watch. We must be having a good time after all! It's two o'clock and we're all used to eating lunch at dead on one!

I raise my voice triumphantly, "Okay everyone, next decent bit of shade we come to we'll stop for lunch."

A feeble cheer goes up.

* * *

There is not a single tree in sight, so we settle for a big arching bush. Ayesha says it's called Broom. Come to think of it the branches do look like witches' brooms. Anyway, it has red and yellow flowers, no prickles, and gives us the shade we need.

"I'm taking me boots off George, and me socks... whoah sorry for the pong!"

"Great idea Smidgin!" All boots and socks are off within seconds and we're laughing about smelly feet and jumping around on the tough wiry turf as if we haven't just trudged for miles and miles with heavy loads on our backs. Smidgin, thank goodness, has forgotten all about her injury and is without a doubt the bounciest of us all!

"Okay Team, get the pack marked "lunch day one" out of your backpacks and then enjoy!"

There are contented *mmms* and *aaaahs* as we tuck into rich and juicy giant sausage rolls. As always there's an appreciative comment from Smidgin, "This is the best meal I've ever 'ad!"

Her comment is usually those very same words so the meals must obviously just keep getting better and better!

But it still has to be said that this time, all of us, including Mikey, make contented chewing sounds of agreement.

After chocolate bars and little apples, we all feel very relaxed, quite sleepy in fact. Mikey and Smidgin are soon curled up, side by side and fast asleep. They look like the babes in the wood.

Now Lloyd gives a contented groan, lies back on the turf, and closes his eyes. He's snoring within a minute.

Ayesha yawns... the most beautiful yawn I've ever heard. Trixie comes and sits by her side and as Ayesha strokes her silky black coat, they are both soon in the land of nod as well.

I stand up, dust the crumbs of food off my clothes and gaze down at my team. Seeing them so peaceful brings an almost painful stab of protectiveness to my body. Shading my eyes from the high sun I scan all around to check for any dangers - was that a person throwing himself down to hide in the heather? Or was it just me over-imagining because I'm just as tired as my friends?  I have to admit I do feel really sleepy.

The sun's still high in the sky. We've got hours and hours before it gets dark and Trixie'll bark if there's any danger near. I need to sleep.

I lie down... this heather makes the springiest sweetest-smelling bed ever... mmmm this is heavenly...

Something about this Scottish air makes me dream. More than anything precise actually happening, this nightmare is about a feeling... an intense atmosphere of menace. Even as I dream, I know this is a warning. It's confirming my suspicions about the figures who are following us. It's throwing me problems about how to keep my friends safe, about whether to continue on the same course or to try to evade the pursuers somehow, by changing direction or finding somewhere to hide.

"Errr Trixie, I did wash this morning thank you." I push her away gently but quickly realise that it's actually really lucky she's woken me up. The sun has gone halfway down the sky since I decided to sleep, and a cool light wind makes me shiver as I recall my nightmare.

Once again, I look hard in every direction. Nothing. Maybe they were just hikers out for a day walk and they've turned around and gone back now. I decide, kind of against my better judgement, to wait until later to talk to Ayesha and Lloyd about my suspicions and for now to "carry on regardless", (as my dad would say).

I clap my hands loudly, sending a few ground-feeding birds into a squawking flurry, "Wake up everyone! We need to get a move on!"

"Oooh Georgie boy you are sooo mean, I was havin' such a nice dream!"

Ayesha yawns and stretches like a sleek and elegant

cat, "What were you dreaming Smidgin?"

"It was about me mam coming to Summerlands. Maggie was teachin' her how to cook."

Mikey accelerates from sound asleep to wide awake in a millisecond. Looking bewildered at his whereabouts for only a moment he's soon scanning all around in a wide-eyed state of high alert.  But Lloyd's slumbering on. Fresh air and exercise are something he still isn't quite used to.

"Mikey, please could you give Lloyd a little shake to wake him up?"

He looks at me doubtfully. I urge him on with a nod and an encouraging raising of my eyebrows. His face explodes into an enormous smile. He creeps over to the sleeping giant, crouches down, shakes his shoulders, and getting no response from that, he tickles Lloyd under the chin then retreats hastily.

Lloyd's response to this stimulation is a monumentally loud fart which wakes him up and makes the rest of us laugh so much that I begin to think we'll never stop. When he asks, "Er… er… did I miss a joke or something?" it only starts us all off again with none of us able to stop for long enough to give him a proper answer.

***

At last all the rucksacks are packed and hoisted onto backs.

"Check the ground around you to make sure nothing's left behind please, and then let's go! Ayesha and Lloyd, can you lead please. We need to go faster than before so we can get to the foot of the mountains to set up camp before dark."

Mikey and Smidgin walk together; not able to talk and giggle quite so much at this faster pace but they're still turning to each other as they go along... and smiling a lot.

I feel like a shepherd because Trixie has chosen to walk by my side to help me keep an eye on the flock. I am reassured that she hasn't shown any sign of awareness of possible pursuers. Surely *she* would know...

***

As the sun gets lower in the sky and the air becomes cooler, the terrain changes. Suddenly there are treacherous sharp rocks to avoid, soggy boggy patches, and little streams to negotiate. Our progress has become worryingly slow.

I'm tired. I feel like skipping the next bit; the finding of the destination, the pitching of the tents, the organising of the meal, the worries I have about possible dangers. What I'd really is like to find that we're suddenly miraculously at the foot of the mountain with the tents set up and the kettle whistling. And with a little daylight left to make it all easy.

I keep looking behind me. Again, I feel sure I saw somebody duck behind a bush about a hundred and fifty metres away. I crouch down to stroke Trixie, smoothing her shiny black head. She looks at me with a "What's the problem?" expression in her eyes.

"Trixie girl, I wish I knew. I'm still hoping there isn't a problem."

I look up and realise that the others are continuing to march on and have got quite far ahead. I decide to put Trixie on her lead and then begin an ungainly wobbly jog across the bumpy boggy ground to catch up.

"Hey you lot, you're getting good at this hiking thing!" I gasp as I reach them.

"Well Georgie boy you know it's gettin' dark and we can't afford to waste any time!" Smidgin quotes my words back at me, and, as always, makes me smile and calms me down.

***

An apologetic rosy golden glow is all the sun is leaving us as it signs off for the day and we approach the looming blackness of the woods.

I'm thinking that the expedition plan drawn up and talked through with all of us in careful detail by John, stated that we should camp about fifty metres from the bottom of the mountains.  We should 've been there by now. Do we even want to enter this dark place tonight? From where I stand, on the edge, the woods look too dense to get through, and by Lloyd's calculations using the Ordnance Survey map, the straightest route is about one and a half kilometres. But the woods will take far longer to cover than a clear path in daylight. And then there are our possible uninvited guests...I feel a rising panic, a cage pressing in on me, tightening relentlessly... this is horribly familiar...but reason tells me that getting angry isn't going to help this time.

I cover my face with my hands, my eyes shut tight. It feels like a kind of refuge, and I start to take some deep breaths.

"Hey George, you okay?"

I find Ayesha by my side looking at me with concern. Because of the kindness in her voice I nearly burst into tears, but I manage to just sniff a bit and rub my nose hard with the back of my hand.

"Ayesha, I feel a bit stressed. I don't know what's the best thing to do right now; it's got so dark already, we should never all have had that sleep." As I say it, it sounds quite funny. Probably it's the worry that starts me off giggling and Ayesha quickly catches the giggles from me.

We are in a possible life or death situation and we're practically crying with laughter. Inappropriate or what!

"Would someone please let me in on the joke?" Lloyd has come over and is looking puzzled and maybe a bit upset at not being in on it.

This causes me to snap back to reality. I look him in the eyes.

"The stupid thing is Lloyd, that there isn't a joke, I was laughing because I'm in a bit of a panic."

"Okay, mate, what's the problem?"

The unexpectedly sympathetic tone of his voice takes

me near to tears again. I cough to clear my throat, "Lloyd mate, we need to discuss our next move."

I look over at Mikey and Smidgin, who are, as usual, lost in each other's company.

I call over to them, "Hey you two, we're taking a break here. Find your torches and keep them safe but don't use them until you have to. Then have a drink and a biscuit from your rations. I need to have a chat with Lloyd and Ayesha."

We sit on the damp heather in a little circle.

"What actually is the matter George? You look terrible." Ayesha looks worried.

"Yeah mate --you do look pretty bad, are you ill?"

"No, I'm just really worried. Together we need to decide about whether we should go into the woods tonight or not."

Suddenly Lloyd becomes an actual different person. Well, maybe not an actual different person, but he does seem to change physically - eyes burning with enthusiasm and a taut upright stance, but even more noticeably, his personality is suddenly assertive and energetic! Wow! I'm glad he's on my side!

"Look man, I've been in this kind of situation over and over in my computer war games. What we need before us are all the relevant facts."

He takes one pace towards me and in an intense Hollywood way he points his   forefinger up and down in time with his speech, "Give...us...the...facts...man!!"

Although I'm totally aware that we're in a very difficult fix right now I still feel the urge to laugh at Lloyd's melodramatic words; but I manage not to.

Looking over at Mikey and Smidgin I can see that she has embarked on one of her long stories. Mikey's giving her his usual rapt attention, so I know they won't be taking any notice of us.

"Lloyd the facts are these. One, John's instructions say that we should camp near to the foot of the mountains, two, that we should have been there and done that before dark, and three, I think we may have been followed since almost the start of the hike."

"Oh George... no wonder you've been looking so worried." Ayesha sounds amazingly calm," but why didn't you tell us before?"

"I thought I might just be imagining it, I thought they might be trekkers like us, or day- hikers who would just turn around and go back before night. I'm not even sure of what I saw now. I didn't want to worry anybody unnecessarily. Everyone was having such a good time. I didn't want to spoil it..." I trail off sadly, finding it such a relief to share my fears that I find that I'm dangerously near to tears.

In an instant Ayesha's giving me a massive hug. After only a slight hesitation Lloyd joins in. I will always remember this hug. It lifts me out of my despair.

Lloyd speaks in his new assertive voice," Right, George, this is the moment when we become a proper unit.

That means sharing all our information and concerns and working together on decision making. Give me a couple of minutes to think about this."

Ayesha and I stare at each other in astonishment at the new improved Lloyd. He catches our expressions, "Look! It's why I'm at Summerlands! My war game addiction. I've been doing cold-turkey."

A little mischievous smile creeps on to his mouth, "And my parents said I was wasting my time playing those games! But I know I can get us out of this guys."

Ayesha speaks for us both, "Wow that is so cool Lloyd!"

## INTO THE WOODS

Minutes later Lloyd looks up from his deliberations; he's been talking to himself under his breath and because he has clicked into war-game thinking. He's been moving his thumbs a lot.

"Yes! Got it!" He turns to us... eyes ablaze.

"Brilliant Lloyd! What's the plan?"

"If it wasn't for your suspicions of being followed, I'd say camp right where we are. But we need to hide - so we have to go into the woods. There's only a bit of light left. We need to get in there right now."

Ayesha gives a little polite cough, "Um-before we move-are we going to tell the little ones about the stalkers?"

"Oh yeah, very good question Ayesha. I think we should wait until we absolutely need to tell them. What do you two think?"

Lloyd considers for a brief moment only, "Yup I agree with you George. It would only make progress more difficult if they're frightened."

Ayesha nods her head thoughtfully, "Good, we're all agreed then!"

She goes over to Smidgin and Mikey to get them moving.

Putting my backpack on I call Trixie. I breathe a sigh of gratitude when she appears at my feet.

"Good girl Trixie, let's put your lead on. You're our guard dog and number one secret weapon now."

Armed with a strong stick for clearing a way through brambles and scrub, Lloyd leads the way. We are in tight formation, single-file. Mikey is after Lloyd, then it's Ayesha, then Smidgin, and me at the end.

It's dark in the woods but the hot air of the day remains, trapped by the trees.  There's a strong smell of disinfectant everywhere, like the stuff they use at school when someone's been sick. Ayesha says it's the scent of the pine-trees.  Whenever we stop still and we're not making our own rustling and crackling sounds we hear the strange and startling noises the forest makes on its own. Trees creak, cones fall to the ground, creatures scuttle near to our feet, and there are sudden loud flappings of wings as the late settlers rise in a panic. It seems you can hear the trees breathe and whisper amongst themselves, like watching giants. For the whole of the day we've been in light and air and space. Now we have to pick our way cautiously, heads down, through a cramped semi-darkness and we know that soon it will be darker still.

Lloyd checked and double-checked the compass before we came into the woods. He kept on flicking it to make sure the needle wasn't stuck. He got Ayesha and me to check it as well, determined to get it right because he wants us out of here as quickly as possible.

Smidgin and Mikey are strangely quiet. This strikes me as weird and a bit scary, but when I think about it I realise that woods nearly always have this effect on people. Because it's so quiet it makes you quiet. I think it is probably one of our human instincts that go back to our primitive past when sabre-tooth tigers, wild boar, and other dangerous animals inhabited the forests. Anyway, it's great that they're being naturally quiet. It means I haven't had to make up stories or explanations.

I'm keeping Trixie on her lead right now. She's more alert and excitable than ever. In this pulling, frantically sniffing, ear-pricking state, surely she will warn us of any danger...

SNAP!

It's so loud in this quiet place that to all of us in our state of high anxiety it sounds like a gun.

"Georgie, Georgie, I'm scared, I want me mam and I need a wee!"

Smidgin is crying. I've only heard angry tears from her before; these tears remind me how young she is and of the massive responsibility I've been given.

Mikey is shaking violently. If I had only just met him, I would think he was having a fit and it would be very alarming. But I know how fearful he is even if I don't know the cause yet.

What would my mum and dad do?

"Group hug everybody!"

As we hold tight together, I think I hear some low muttering a small distance away but none of the others do, including, most importantly, Trixie... I must be imagining it. These woods really do have a life of their own.

"Sorry to make you jump everybody, I stepped onto a very large twig. It hurt a bit actually." Lloyd sounds properly apologetic, and quite sorry for himself as well.

Ayesha, as always, has the right words, the comforting voice, "That's alright Lloyd, I was falling asleep on my feet and I needed waking up. Now Smidgin, let's find a nice bush toilet before we wet ourselves!"

Smidgin giggles.

"Don't go far, Ayesha!" I feel real horror rising at the thought of them going anywhere, "In fact, just step away a bit and us boys will keep our eyes shut until you say we can open them."

"Okay boys, thank you, we'll do the same for you anytime, won't we Smidgin?"

Smidgin will never lose her mischievous sense of humour, "Well... we might peep a tiny little bit."

***

The plan now is to find just enough space between trees to pitch the two tents close together.

It's beginning to look like we'll never find that perfect spot when we come to a space even bigger than we need. It's a clearing. I look up and see past the scarily tall trees to a bright half-moon and stars which are, unbelievably, shining even more brightly than the ones I saw when I went out for that walk with Trixie.

"We'll pitch the tents at the edge here." Lloyd has taken over leadership of the team for a while, without any discussion, and it feels natural and right. He, after all, is the expert on jungle warfare and survival.

"First clear your area of any big rocks or sticks, then go for it," he says, echoing John's exact words when we were training.

As I watch the expert tent- erecting group that Team George turns out to be,

I almost forget that nagging, dragging sense of doom that's been pulling me down all day.

"Look what we've done Team, even in the dark! I can't believe how clever we are! Well done everyone! Now we can eat!"

Lloyd sets the stove up to make tea and Ayesha helps Smidgin and Mikey sort out Trixie's food and water. For "Supper Day One" there are massive cheese and onion pasties, hunks of fruitcake, and a satsuma each.

We sit round the stove eating in silence, apart that is from a few "*Mmmms*" and "*Aaahs*" and "*Yummms*".

"That," Ayesha announces with great solemnity, "Was by far the best meal I've ever had."

Smidgin's nodding enthusiastically, "Yeah I 'ave to agree with you on that one Ayesha. A little round of applause for Maggie is called for I think!"

I look round at all my friends as they smile and clap... and see that Mikey's struggling to keep his eyes open.

"Mikey, it's time for you to hit the sack I think."

He looks at me uncomprehendingly. Smidgin catches the look, "George means it's time for bed Mikey."

He smiles his famous smile then immediately looks dead scared.

"It's alright Mikey, we'll keep you safe. You are going to sleep between me and Lloyd in the boys' tent."

Even as I hold a torch for him to settle into his sleeping -bag he falls asleep.

Ayesha crawls silently out of the girls' tent, "That's two down then," she beams.

"Yup, Mikey literally went out like a light too! Time for one more cuppa!"

## THE NIGHT WATCH

It's colder now, and damp. We sit warming our hands round the hot mugs.

"Lloyd, what do you think about keeping guard during the night?"

I'm almost hoping he'll say no need. I'm finding it difficult to stay awake. I can't remember feeling this tired ever in my whole life. But his reply is a passionate,

"Yes, yes, yes and yes George; in my war games my life has been saved seven times by a soldier on sentry duty! We'll take it in turns."

Ayesha has been watching me yawning. "Can I take first watch Lloyd? I'm not at all sleepy."

"Okay Ayesha. Time check George?"

"It's coming up to 11pm."

"Right Ayesha, can you do until 1am then wake me and I'll do until 3am. Then George it'll be your turn until reveille - that's waking up time!"

"You'll need the watch Ayesha!"

"Thanks George. Goodnight you two."

***

"Oh no Lloyd, is it really my turn already? Are you absolutely certain?"

"Yes George, I am certain. Ayesha's done her watch,

I've done mine! It's your turn to wake up and my turn to go to sleep again."

"Alright, alright - no need to shout!"

"George, I am not shouting actually."

"Oh yeah, sorry Lloyd, it just feels like it because I really don't want to get up."

"Anyway George, you'll be pleased to hear that there hasn't been anything to worry about so far. Trixie's sleeping like a log."

"Thanks Lloyd, I'll get on with it now. Have a good sleep."

***

It's really cold out here. I get my coat on and zip it right up. I sit close to Trixie for warmth and reassurance.

I bend down and whisper in her ear, "Now don't sleep too deeply Trixie girl, we need you to be a Rottweiler now." She turns her head, licks my face, yuk! And goes right back to sleep.

Looks like I'm on my own then. You wouldn't think that the sounds of a forest would be so loud. What with the flapping of the tents, the trees creaking, the snuffling of hedgehogs, the bovver-booted forest mice scuttling in the undergrowth, and to cap it all, that owl hooting right over my head. That sound would have been really spooky if it wasn't for all the other noises...

***

Nice and warm now and getting used to the strange soundtrack of the forest, I'm nodding off slightly when I become aware of a low growly moan coming from Trixie's throat...

Immediately I'm wide- awake, senses straining, heart racing. I narrow my eyes to scan all around me. I know that if I can catch sight of them, they will probably be able to see me. Oh no! Two shadowy human shapes are about a hundred metres away. It looks like they're coming this way.

Will they be able to see us? We're right at the edge of the clearing, in shadow.

"Keep still Trixie, keep quiet," I whisper, stroking her head, "Please, please please...

My heart's beating so fast and so loud that I think they might hear it.

In the first weak light of dawn I see them. One is a very tall skinny white guy, he slouches and shambles along. He reminds me of that guy in the Scooby-doo cartoons - Shaggy. The other is black, an average kind of height, and he just seems much more alert than his mate, who really looks like he's lost it.

They're mumbling in low voices but with my currently acute hearing I make out snatches..." They must be in here somewhere...if we don't get that kid it'll be us instead...I'm knackered why the...didn't we bring food... let's kip now. We'll find them easy when it's light ..."

\*\*\*

"Lloyd, wake up, wake up now!" I'm whispering forcefully into his ear but he's flat out, I shake his shoulder. Suddenly he shouts, "Mobilise, mobilise!"

Now that *really* makes me jump!

"Shush Lloyd, shush. This isn't a game!  We've gotta get away from here fast. I've seen the enemy. There're two of them. They haven't seen us yet but I reckon they might if we don't move quickly.  Okay Lloyd? You wake Mikey up and I'll get the girls moving."

The girls must've heard Lloyd yelling. They're already starting to pack up.

"Alright Ayesha? Alright Smidgin? We're moving out as quickly and quietly as we can."

"What's goin' on Georgie boy?"

I exchange a brief look with Ayesha that means *"should I tell Smidgin now?"*

Ayesha replies with a tiny frown and an almost imperceptible shake of the head.

"We need to make up for lost time Smidgin, there's no time for talking."

"Aw Georgie, how can you expect me to not talk?"

I smile but I don't answer.

"That's brilliant work you two!" Lloyd and Mikey are just bagging the boys' tent. "Good job well done," as my dad would say.

"We've finished too- oo, we were very qu- ick," Smidgin sings.

"That, Smidgin, is because you didn't talk while you were doing it. Right everyone, grab a drink of water and a biscuit and we're outta here. Lloyd, got the compass?"

"Yes sir! We are heading due north sir!"

Because of the need for speed we've split Mikey and Smidgin up, so Mikey's at the front with Lloyd, Smidgin's with Ayesha in the middle, and I'm the rear guard again.

I look behind to check nothing's left on the ground. There's something there. I go back. It's Trixie's lead. I'd forgotten all about her. Somebody must have let her off for a run! My heart sinks. I feel sick, but I know that we just have to go on and hope she'll find us.

I pocket the lead and do a shambling jog to catch up with the others, "You okay up there Lloyd, are we still going due north?"

"Yes George, you can rely on that. I have the compass in my hand!"

"You alright Ayesha?"

"Yes, thanks George, I've never been better!" she answers in her bright-as-the-morning voice. And then I catch her saying quietly to herself, "Well not for a very long time that is."

"What about you Smidgin? Is your ankle okay?"

"Ooo yes I'm great thanks, good as new Georgie boy. I am 'avin' the 'oliday of a lifetime don't you know!"

"And Mikey," I call, "Are you feeling good?"

His answer is to turn around to face me with a fierce look, and his finger on his lips to warn me to be quiet.

## FACE TO FACE

The sun's up now, sharp light cutting between the trees and dazzling white on the forest floor. I feel a bit calmer now because I'm fairly certain we have some distance between us and the enemy.

"Lloyd, have you checked the compass recently? We've been walking quite fast for over an hour now."

"Affirmative George, we have totally been travelling due north the whole time."

"Yeah of course Lloyd, sorry, you do know I trust you completely. How much longer do you think it'll take? I just want to be out of these woods. Get some daylight around us."

"According to my calculations, about twenty minutes, barring any unforeseen circumstances that is."

Ayesha laughs, her glorious pealing laugh, like a magic woodland spirit, "We don't need any of those horrible things, do we?"

Smidgin pipes up, "What don't we need Ayesha? Any what horrible things?"

Lloyd, Ayesha, and me all answer together, as one, "Unforeseen circumstances!"

Suddenly we're all laughing together, on that never-ending roll, where you think you can stop then you catch someone's eye, or a little giggle comes up through your throat and you're all off again.

And then I look at Mikey and I know that he's in no fit state to see the funny side of anything.

"Okay team, let's hit the road again!"

Climbing over fallen trees, tripping on smaller branches, stung by snapping twigs, cut by thorns, falling in soggy ditches, I'm going off woodland walks more and more by the minute. I hope we don't have to come back this way...

"Are we nearly there yet?"

Smidgin has only asked this question about six hundred times over the last forty-five minutes. To be fair I know exactly how she feels; she just wants to get out of this damp and dismal difficult place and into the light.

Suddenly there's a rushing crushing crashing bashing behind us. It shakes us with its loudness and unexpectedness. We all look behind, except for Mikey who throws himself down and rolls into a tight ball.

"Oh Trixie, it's you! Thank goodness you're here." I'm crouching down hugging her, not caring that she's giving me one of those thorough face washes which I really don't like.

"Trixie what's this?" I whisper, realising that she has a tiny rolled- up piece of paper attached to her collar. My heart's beating fast and loud as I quickly and carefully get it off and tuck it into my pocket.

"Okay, now we've got our guard dog back let's go a bit faster and get out of here." I'm hoping they don't notice the wobble I feel in my voice. "Lloyd are you keeping an eye on that compass?"

"Are you doubting me Captain George sir?" he jokes, "I can actually see the light at the end of the woods now. Five minutes and we'll be out of here everybody, then we'll stop for a breather."

***

The light outside of the woods is dazzling. It's one of those white-cloud days when the brilliance of the sun is diffused across the whole sky. We all take a deep breath at the same moment, but no one smiles.

We sit together in a huddle close to the trees.

"Can you all get a drink now. And have just one biscuit this time. We might need to make our food last longer than planned."

"Why Georgie boy?" Smidgin always wants to know why. I have to think on my feet with her.

"It's because we're running behind schedule, because of that long nap we all had during the day yesterday Smidgin."

I feel for the bit of paper in my pocket; I turn away from the group as I unroll it. Four words scratched on a cigarette paper. I can just make them out.

"WE WILL GET HIM"

"What's wrong George? You're as white as a sheet."

"Ayesha I need to have a quick word with you and

Lloyd"

Lloyd's standing near and he hears me, "Yes boss, what's the problem?"

I glance at Smidgin and Mikey. They're throwing a stick for Trixie to fetch, too busy to take any notice of us.

I get the malevolent message out of my pocket and hold it out for Ayesha and Lloyd to see.

Lloyd at once becomes reassuringly business-like, "Where did you find this George?"

"It was tucked into the buckle of Trixie's collar when she came back after spending the night away."

"So, if there's someone stalking us George, which of us are they after?"

Ayesha's looking more than a bit frightened, "I suppose it must be one of the boys, it says "HIM." "

"I don't think I can have any real-life enemies," Lloyd is speaking in his military-type voice, I haven't hardly left my bedroom for about three years, let alone my house. I've been completely imprisoned by computer war games. I don't see how I can have upset anyone."

"I can't really think of why I would be a target either, unless the teacher I hit wants to get his own back!" I giggle a bit madly at the thought.

Ayesha suddenly realises who the intended victim is. Her eyes widen with realisation and tears roll down her cheeks. "Oh no it's little Mikey isn't it!"

I put my arm round her shoulder. "We'll look after him Ayesha; we'll all look after him."

Smidgin has noticed Ayesha's distress "Wha's wrong Ayesha?"

"I...I'm a bit homesick all of a sudden Smidgin, I'll be all right in a minute. Thank you for asking."

Smidgin leaves Mikey's side to come over and give Ayesha a massive hug. Then she wipes Ayesha's tears from her cheeks with tiny grubby fingers as she looks searchingly into her eyes. "It'll be alright, you'll soon be home with your mam. And remember you've got all of us to you keep you company in the meantime."

Ayesha sniffs in deeply, smiles a bit sadly, and kisses Smidgin on the cheek.

"Smidgin you are amazing and I love you to bits."

Content that she has comforted Ayesha, Smidgin gets back to Mikey. They are instantly back in their own private magical world.  Now we have to get back to the serious stuff.

"We need to move fast but we must have a proper plan of action." I say. "Lloyd, how are we going to get out of this?"

Lloyd's on it," First priority is the safety of Mikey. I personally will take responsibility for him. He will stay with me at all times until this is over. Ayesha, you will keep Smidgin with you. George, you will oversee the whole group as you have been doing.

We don't know where the enemy is. We need to

move fast. We have to dump all our equipment bar the absolute essentials."

I'm listening intently to Lloyd, but I suddenly become aware of a scuffling noise and a low muttering, then the snap of a broken twig away in the forest. Trixie's growling deeply, her ears are pricked up and her eyes are looking in the direction of the sounds.

"Lloyd! did you hear that? Wide-eyed, he nods in answer." But they don't know we're here. Smidgin, quietly, Mikey, grab your things, back into the woods!"

***

We huddle in a tight bunch a few meters into the trees. All our gear is in a pile nearer to the edge. Our hearts all beating loudly together sound like a massive drum.

I'm holding Trixie in the circle. She's whimpering and struggling but I can't let her go. She would give us away instantly.

Suddenly I find myself giving orders in the hiss of an aggressive stage whisper. "Smidgin, Mikey and Ayesha, listen carefully. You must go deeper into the woods, but not too far- you must be able to get back here and not get lost. Go very quietly, find somewhere to hide and stay there till we come to get you. Trixie'll help us sniff you out. Any questions?"

Smidgin ,as always, has a question, "Warra we hiding from?"

"Good question Smidgin. The answer is we're not

really sure. We think it's two not very nice men. Okay? Now go as quietly as you can. Go!"

I point them in the direction I want them to go. I whisper, "Not too far and keep very quiet."

Ayesha looks back worriedly as she shepherds Mikey and Smidgin out of sight.

"Right Lloyd, I hope that was the right thing to do but we just didn't have time to think about it with the enemy being so near."

Lloyd opens his mouth to speak, but at the same time an arm is clamped round his neck. Springing up to defend him I release Trixie. She barks, growls, and bites at the legs of the assailant who maintains his grip on Lloyd whilst kicking angrily and viciously at her.

I figure that I must be stronger than this tall skinny gangly guy. With Trixie undeterred from her attack, though yelping with pain at every kick, I can easily get Lloyd free.

I get to three on my mental countdown and I'm ready to attack when suddenly it's my turn to be clamped round the neck.

I try to speak but each time a sound comes out of my mouth the guy tightens his grip. It feels like he could easily kill me, so I stop trying.

The tall skinny guy, the one who's like Shaggy, shouts in a strange squeaky voice, "Get this stupid animal off me or I will put this blade in it."

He pulls a shiny curved six-inch knife from his parka

pocket.

I manage to call Trixie off, she drops to the ground in the sheepdog holding position, growling in that continuous low tone.

The guy who's holding me is very strong and stocky - he seems to be the boss here, much more sure of himself than Shaggy, who now asks for orders. "What do I do with this one Leo?"

"Don't use my name you idiot! Tie him to a tree. I'll see to this one if that one tries anything."

I feel cold steel held to my neck. This can't be real can it? I keep very still and watch whilst Shaggy makes Lloyd stand with his back against a tree with his arms behind the trunk. Shaggy savagely yanks Lloyd's wrists together and ties them with what looks like a silk bandana. Then he ties another silk scarf, or something like it, round Lloyd's open mouth. Lloyd's eyes are bulging out of his head with fear, but he makes no sound.

"Man - you made such a good job of that one you can do this one too!"

Shaggy looks so happy with the praise that, for a nanosecond, I feel a bit sad for him.

Leo's holding Lloyd's chin up with one hand and a knife to his throat with the other whilst Shaggy ties me up.

"Na don't gag him yet. He's got to talk." Leo puts his face so close to mine that I can feel the heat and the evaporating sweat from it - "haven't you?"

"Have I?" Now Leo headbutts me so that my head bangs into the tree and then grabbing on to my hair he grinds my head on the rough bark. I feel a warm trickle of blood run down my face.

"You a bit of a smartarse?"

I just can't help answering back even though I know I'm probably going to suffer for it - "What me?"

"That's enough smartarse, you'd better be smart enough to tell me where the kid is or your long-haired friend here is going to feel a lot of pain - or worse!"

I glance over at Lloyd who looks close to collapsing with fear but still he's trying to tell me with his eyes not to speak.

I'm trying to work out in my hurting head whether to mess about and delay them or simply send them in the wrong direction. I think I'll delay a bit and risk them losing it and hurting us.

"So? Where is he then?"

"Who?"

"Hold that blade on the emo's cheek mate, this friend of his wants to play silly beggars. We'll show him we're not playin.'

"Alright alright," I yell, "but why do you want Mikey? He's just a little kid on holiday. Why do you want him? He can't even speak."

"Can't speak? What do you mean he can't speak?

Course he can speak."

"We've never heard him speak, have we Lloyd?"

Shaggy takes off the gag to let him answer and stands back,

"No,  Mikey's completely dumb!"

As Shaggy ties the gag back on Lloyd he suddenly becomes very excited,

"Leo, Leo!"

"Don't use my name you stupid idiot, how many times have I told you?"

"Sorry, sorry, sorry mate, I'm really sorry. It's just, just that if the kid can't talk, he can't give no evidence can 'e? That means we don't 'ave to do 'im in don't it?"

"He can still write you div, he can write a statement can't he? If Kimo goes down, we're as good as dead!  You just don't get it do you?"

"I don't want to kill no-one. Can't we just get 'old of 'im an' put the frighteners on?  Couldn't we just do that and then run off?  Somewhere else.  Not go back to London?"

"We came all this way to get him, you know that, and I've called for back-up now. ,Come on, just make sure these can't get away and we'll go and dig that kid out." Leo puts his face to mine again," Which way did he go? Tell me the truth or you and pretty boy here will both suffer when we get back."

I know I can't mess with them anymore, they're both getting dangerously wound-up. Clearly, they are as scared as us. Do I double-bluff, telling them the right direction because they'll think I'll say the wrong direction?

I decide to tell them the right direction, "They're over there somewhere." I nod my head that way.

"You think we're stupid, don't you? Come on you!"

They go off in the opposite direction to what I told them. Luckily, they forget to gag me.

## OUT OF THE WOODS

I wait a few minutes, 'til I can't hear them anymore and then turn to Lloyd,

"You okay mate?"

He nods, the colour is already coming back to his face thank goodness.

"That last five minutes was a bit of an ordeal Lloyd, sorry I kept provoking them. I just hope it gave Mikey and the girls time to get themselves to safety somehow.  It doesn't look as though we'll be much use to them. I feel like the more I wriggle my hands the tighter the knot gets. It'll take a miracle to get us out of here."

"Call me Little Miss Miracle then!"

"Oh Smidgin!" She's untying the knot with tiny hot fingers. Ayesha's untying Lloyd's hands; Mikey hugs first me and then Lloyd.

"I hate to break up the peace and love thing," Lloyd's back in control," but we need to get out of here now! Get Trixie on her lead, put your backpacks on and follow me. Don't run, we can't afford any accidents, but walk as fast as you can and keep together!"

Lloyd checks the ground to make sure we haven't left anything important then storms off. He stops after a few paces turns around and speaks in a fierce loud stage whisper.  "Follow me and be quiet!"

Everyone falls into line without hesitation.

Mikey is directly behind Lloyd, then Smidgin, then Ayesha. I take up the rear with Trixie.

"I'm really scared George," Ayesha is whispering, and her wide eyes are showing her fear even more clearly than her words.

"Me too Ayesha, but we must keep our heads and trust in Lloyd's skills," I whisper back, "Come on, we have to do this!"

Now we fall back into our own thoughts as we tread on as quietly as we can. Every now and then there's a stumble or an ouch from Mikey or Smidgin but they definitely understand the urgency of this particular hike and they don't let anything slow them down.

All of a sudden Lloyd stops and turns to face us. He talks fast and breathlessly, "I can see light; we're nearly at the edge of the forest. Keep a few paces behind me so I can make sure the way is clear before you all follow."

Now he creeps on all-fours. It looks strange; then I remember the war games I used to play with my friends in the woods, and crawling just like that to be as hidden as possible. He beckons and nods his head slowly to tell us to come forward slowly.

As we come out of the woods once more, we see the sun shining in a now blue sky; its warmth on our faces is like a blessing. There's not much time to enjoy it though; Lloyd's ready to give us our next briefing.

"Right team, we've done extremely well so far, but our next challenge is going to be even bigger. I expect you've noticed that mountain over there!"

We all laugh. Lloyd doesn't often make jokes, so we really appreciate this.

"Well, we are going to have to get to the other side of it. And fast. When we leave the edge of these woods, we are going to be highly visible to the enemy, so we have to be really quick. We need to leave our rucksacks now. Get your survival blankets and torches, plus as much food and water as you can fit in your pockets."

"But John and Maggie said we mustn't do any mountain climbing!" Smidgin sounds really worried. Lloyd looks a bit unsure about what to say so I speak up quickly.

"Something unexpected has come up." I explain. "We need to take a bit of a detour to get back to base safely. It'll be more mountain walking than climbing anyway. We've all just got to trust Lloyd and do exactly what he says."

"But, but..."

"No time for talking Smidgin, we need to go now!"

Lloyd takes over again, "Right, stash the rucksacks here out of sight just inside the woods, then run for it. On my count of three – one, two, three -RUN!"

I reckon it's about two hundred metres, a sprint in athletics, and we're all sprinting now, same order as before, Lloyd out in front setting the pace.

We all reach the base of the mountain in about one-minute flat. We're all a completely out of breath. Between taking gulps of air, Lloyd issues his next orders.

"Good run everyone! Now stay low and listen up. We've got to cross this mountain as fast as possible, okay?"

We all look up at the mountain with wonder and fear. It looks big and steep and mean. Some of it is bare rock, other parts have a sandy white soil, and it is scattered with scratchy little bushes and scrubby grass.

"Don't be scared," Lloyd urges, "You have to think of this mountain as your friend. It's going to keep us safe. The plan is not to climb to the top and down the other side. We're going to skirt it. Not going even halfway up. All got your breath back? Follow me and keep tight together!"

Ayesha and I look at each other with raised eyebrows and grateful smiles for the new knowledgeable and dynamic Lloyd as we follow his lead on to the left side of the mountain.

## THE MOUNTAIN

I've never done any mountain walking before. It's tough. You have to kind of lean into the side a lot of the time. Lloyd looks as if he's really experienced at it. Mikey and Smidgin have already worked out how to do it. I think it's just me and Ayesha who're struggling. In spite of the walking boots with their grippy heavy treads we're slipping quite a lot.

Trixie must be very fed up with the tugs she gets on her lead every time I lose my footing, but she doesn't complain.

"We're going to have a breather now," Lloyd announces, "See that clump of bushes just ahead? We'll stop there for ten minutes max to rest our legs and have a drink."

What a relief. This mountain is definitely larger than it looks. We all get behind the only- just- big- enough screen of shrubbery and sit looking back at the ground we've covered.

"Get your drinks but remember to leave some water in your bottles. We may find a clear stream that we can drink from, but we may not."

I am so impressed. Lloyd certainly seems to have all areas covered. And he's good at giving orders. Now he shades his eyes and peers into the distance.

"They're there!"

He's pointing back towards the edge of the woods where there are what look like two evil gnomes doing a weird mad dance of rage. It looks like they've found the kit that we dumped and now they're knifing it, tearing it apart, jumping and stamping on it and throwing it in the air.

"I'm afraid we're stuck here for a bit guys," Lloyd announces in a very relaxed way, "If we can see them, they'll definitely be able to see us if we break cover."

"But Lloyd," Smidgin can't help quipping, "If we break wind, they'll be able to smell us!"

We all laugh, but quietly. Even Mikey giggles a bit.

"Very funny Smidgin," Lloyd concedes; "But now listen carefully, because we're in quite a tricky situation here. We all need to be as still as we can, and George, you'll have to make sure Trixie doesn't wriggle out of position. Any questions?"

It is, of course, Smidgin who asks, "Lloyd, how long will we have to wait here?"

"Good question Smidgin, but I don't know the answer. We'll have to watch and see which way they go. We may have to wait until dark."

As soon as the two younger ones become immersed in one of their deep and seemingly highly confidential conversations, Lloyd gets me and Ayesha in a huddle to discuss what we might do next.

"By what we heard the enemy say it seems they might be getting reinforcements up here; that means that we can't afford to hang around anymore than is absolutely necessary." he whispers.

Ayesha says what I'm thinking, "I don't know if I'm being thick Lloyd, but isn't that kind of what we need to do anyway?"

"Ayesha I take your point, yes of course we want to get to safety as quickly as possible, but I want to emphasise the need for speed at this point because although we can be pretty sure these current guys have only knives, I think their mates may come with guns."

This comes as a massive shock to me, but I quickly realise that Lloyd is probably right. This tracking game is deadly serious in every way.

"Lloyd, it looks like they're ready to move!"

I've been watching the enemy the whole time. They've been sitting on the ground close together, talking by the look of it.  Now they stand up and shake hands energetically.

"I think they're going to split up George," Lloyd whispers, " that could be a mixed blessing. Good for us if we can capture them one by one, bad because they stand more chance of finding us faster. And we don't know how close their mates might be."

* * *

Sure enough, they split up. The tall skinny one seems to be following the route that we've come; the other one's taking the other side of the mountain.

"What d'you think Lloyd?" Ayesha's almost squeaking she's so frightened, "Are we going to sit tight or run for it?"

"We can wait a minute or two longer- he may not stay on that trajectory."

Lloyd sounds so calm and confident.

And he's right. I swear Lloyd is opening his mouth and taking a deep breath ready to give orders to run when suddenly Shaggy stands still, and, shading his eyes with his hand, slowly looks all around. His gaze seems to linger on our hiding place much longer than feels comfortable. We all hold our breath, and we can hear our hearts pounding... but he can't have spotted us because now he's stepping downwards to go on a lower path.

"Lloyd! Well done! How did you know mate?"

"Like I said before George, when you've played as many rounds of Ace War Strategy games as me you really should have some idea of what might happen."

Ayesha pats him enthusiastically on the back, "Well done Lloyd! We are so lucky we've got you to steer us through this mess. What's the next move?"

"The next move, Ayesha, is to stay still. Until dark. Which," he says, looking towards the sun which is now low in the sky, "will be in around three hours max I reckon."

"Okay Lloyd, I'll tell Mikey and Smidgin what's happening. "

"I'll talk to them as well Ayesha."

Mikey and Smidgin have been as good as gold in the safe little world they've constructed together. But right now, they're not completely aware of the danger we're in.

I watch as Lloyd and Ayesha huddle with Smidgin and Mikey. A gentle golden beam of the setting sun lights them. The scene reminds me of the family sitting around the table in my dream at the croft. So peaceful and loving. I'm suddenly stabbed again by that overwhelming feeling of protectiveness; I know I will stop at nothing to keep my new family safe.

## THE HIGHLANDERS

It's very dark when I'm awoken by Trixie's low throaty growling. I put my hand on her head to reassure and quieten her. But she's too worried to stop. At least it's a very quiet warning. My eyes quickly adjust to the darkness. I look over at the others, all in a huddle and fast asleep.

Now Trixie sits up, ears pricked, on full alert. I strain my ears and hear a rustling and murmuring. In the deep silence of the mountainside these sounds could come from more than a hundred metres away.

I see small lights flashing, the distance between them increasing gradually. They know where we are. They're moving to surround us. To trap us...

"Wake up Lloyd! Ayesha wake up! They're here. I think there are five of them!"

Lloyd seems slow to react, but I know he's clicked in to the situation straightaway. I can see that his brain is working by the way his eyes are moving.

"Ayesha wake the children up, as quietly as you can. Tell them they'll be fine, but they have to be ready to go when I give the order. George I'm volunteering you to be last out of here. You'll be covering our backs so we can get a head start."

Mikey and Smidgin are rubbing their eyes and yawning as Ayesha brings them into the circle.

"Right guys you need to be awake right now!"

The two young ones react immediately. I think they

know instinctively what danger we're in. They're fully awake and practically standing to attention.

"Listen up, here's the plan! Ayesha, you're first to go with Smidgin. That way!"

Lloyd is pointing down the mountain to the right.

"I'm looking after you Mikey. We'll go nearly the same way as Ayesha and Smidgin, but not exactly, so we make it harder for the enemy. Stick right by me Mikey."

Mikey flinches and frowns but he nods wide-eyed and energetically.

"George will help our escape by distraction techniques." Lloyd turns to me, "The first one, George, is to throw rocks in varied directions, to confuse them. It'll buy us some time. The second one is, just before you run for it, to start a scrub fire. Just set fire to the nearest dry vegetation. I'm pretty confident it'll spread fast. Got the matches George?"

"Yes Lloyd," I answer as I pat my pocket to make sure they're there.

"Ready with the rocks? Start throwing now!"

I've got ten golf-ball sized rocks by my side on the ground. I throw the first as far as I can to my right.

Lloyd says, "Ayesha and Smidgen go, go, GO!"

They fly off into the darkness as I throw my second stone, "We're off now George, good luck! Come on Mikey!"

As I throw my third stone they too fly off into the darkness.

I try to locate the five torchlights. I see only two. They're moving in the direction that I've been sending the stones. That means that at least two of the enemy are not near my team. Where are the other three? Could be anywhere! I'll just finish lobbing these rocks till I run out. I'll send number nine directly in front, straight down the hill...

"Aah, ow, get off! what are you doing? Ow!"

There's a massive arm clamped round my neck! I can't breathe! Uh oh - déjà vu!

Thank goodness Trixie's here, snarling and snapping at the attacker's legs. Keep going Trixie girl, keep going...The man is kicking out at her and sometimes she yelps in pain but she just keeps going. The grip round my neck loosens - I'm able to strike a match and drop it onto the dry bush below. It crackles briefly then bursts into flames. The man is completely bewildered for a split second but I don't move fast enough. He grabs my arm. I kick him in the shin. This time I run for it...

I don't look back. The mountainside is fast lighting up with fire, I see all of my team being pursued-running for their lives - my heart's sinking...

BANG! That's a gunshot echoing on the mountain! This could mean the end...*please let my friends be safe*.

Now another unfamiliar sound...I think it's bagpipes...

I stop running to look behind me. What I see I can

hardly believe. Emerging from the smoke, following the piper, are eight huge men with grey kilts swirling and long wild hair flying. They brandish massive swords. The piper carries on marching and playing as the other highlanders holler loudly and break into a surefooted run towards my friends... and the enemy.

As the warriors get nearer to me, I can see that one is smaller and younger than the others. He looks very familiar; he looks like the boy from my dream at the croft.

His face shines with courage. He looks at me, confused at first and then smiling broadly. He breaks ranks to run to me. Now it's me who's bewildered.

The boy holds out his hand to shake, as we do so he lands a heavy pat on my shoulder.

"Rory's the name!"

"I'm George." I manage to squeak.

"George is it? However did ye manage tae get yourself into such a predicament?"

"Er - er... long story..."

Not waiting even half a second for the story Rory grabs my hand and pulls me with him into the chase.

The other warriors are storming down the mountainside and we're running to catch them up. As we run, I feel an explosion within me... an overwhelming conviction that tells me I can do this. I find myself hollering like the warriors! I *am* a warrior!

Now the highlanders are scattered ahead of Rory and me. The enemy are outnumbered. It looks clear who's going to win this battle.

But - oh no! By a sudden high flame in the scrub fire I see one of the enemy closing down on Mikey...no warriors near them...I see a gun in the enemy's hand. I'm terrified for Mikey. A bloodcurdling wail fills the mountainside as I prepare for the sprint of my life.

"Go George, go!" Rory's at my side.

Brothers in arms...flying...now I can't see Rory... he's not here... but I can still feel his power... his strength... I've become him.

I find myself in a massive dive catching the legs of Shaggy and landing him on the ground with a thud! I grab the gun, and somehow I know how to check the safety catch before passing it to Mikey. Shaggy is kind of dazed, I think the thud was his head, so it's easy to kneel on his back and tie his hands with the tartan bandana I find in my pocket.

"You got him George. You really got him!"

I look up from tying Shaggy's feet together;" You spoke Mikey. You really spoke!"

He springs over to me and we hug. We look across the burning mountainside and see two more of the enemy on the ground. They are being bound up by our warriors. That means there are two left to deal with.

Chasing Lloyd man on man through the burning scrub

one of the two comes into sight. Suddenly Lloyd stops, turns on his pursuer and lands a massive blow to his stomach. Now Lloyd slaps his face, grabs his arms and pulls them behind his back. As if by magic a warrior appears and passes Lloyd a rope to tie the shocked man up.

One more villain left then...

"George!" Mikey's screaming...I turn round. It looks like an ogre - head huge - face grim. He stands staring down at us. We stare at him.

"Mikey pass the gun!"

Mikey's quick...but before I've even pointed the gun at the ogre, he's lunging at me and I'm on the ground. He snatches the gun from my hand, stands back and points it at Mikey.

I see my brain turn dark red as I scream, "Nooo...Nooo...Never"

But wait. The safety catch is on. I do the first thing that comes into my head. I bite his leg. He grunts with pain, but he still has the gun...and he's still staring at Mikey.

Keeping his eyes on Mikey he checks the gun and releases the safety catch. He looks soulless – cold - like an executioner. Will he do it? *Can* he do it? Can he kill a child who's trembling and calling for his mother? I'll never know because the ogre is suddenly felled by a fast-flying missile that hits him from behind catching him off-balance... Trixie!

"Run Mikey! run for your life!" I manage to gasp.

Why don't I go with him?

Having brought her prey down Trixie hurls herself on to him, snarling, growling, biting. But he pushes her off gets to his feet and fires a shot. She slumps to the ground.

Blind with rage, I fly at the ogre, punching, kicking, screaming, crying. He still has the gun. I don't care. He catches me round the neck and holds it to my head...

\*\*\*

"Wake up braw laddie ye need tae get tae your hame noo..."

I'm finding it hard to work out where I am...the voice...sounds like John...am I back at Summerlands?  I need to lie a bit longer. I feel scared about what I might wake up to.

"Come on now laddie ye must open your eyes noo."

He seems to know that I'm choosing whether to come back or not.

"All will be well... wake up noo."

His voice is gruff but gentle. I feel like when I was little, and my dad would wake me from a nightmare.

Slowly...very slowly... I open my eyes.

It's a warrior, red hair, red beard, red and kindly face. Lying on the ground behind him is a huge grunting tied-up bundle. It's the ogre.

"I'm alive...you saved me...thank you."

"Och laddie ye put up quite a fight yeself. We gave ye

a wee bit o' support that's all."

I'm still feeling dazed...a bit weak... not quite fully conscious...I try to stand up...I can't...

"Sit a wee while longer laddie."

Now I panic... I hear myself whispering," Mikey? Trixie?"

"Mikey - we have him. He's safe, fine and dandy. But who is Trixie? Have we missed someone?"

"Trixie, she's a sheepdog. Where is she?" I'm sobbing violently. Out of control.

I'm embraced in a massive rough and smelly hug.

"Och laddie, if ye love her that much she won't be far. Call her...she'll come."

Now my new friend stands up and thumps my back heartily. Then he turns away and strides upwards to the thick grey mist where I can just make out the other warriors. As they disappear, I see Rory stop and turn to look back at me. He raises his hand high in farewell. Behind them they leave the sound of the bagpipes which becomes ever fainter until I know it's left only in my mind and soul.

* * *

It's light now. I'm near the foot of the mountain. My team are all running towards me.

Behind them masses of blue lights flash. There's a lot of activity down there.

As my friends get nearer, I manage to stand up. I call out for Trixie. I hear a weak yelping kind of bark! I turn to see her limping painfully down the slope towards me. That bullet must have hit her leg.

"Oh Trixie!" I'm crying again as I hug her beautiful smelly matted neck. She licks my face. I look up and see all my friends in a tight circle around us.

# EPILOGUE

*The story has been passed down through many generations of both the McGlade and the McGregor clans.*

*No doubt there are some differences in the accounts depending upon whether it is a McGlade or a McGregor telling it:*

*For many decades the clans had been living side by side in peace... until a misunderstanding upset everything.*

*Each year in late spring the sheep which grazed freely on the mountainsides and heathland would be gathered in for the purposes of counting, shearing, marking and checking for health.*

*Newborn lambs would be marked whilst they were still with their mothers, McGlade lambs were marked with red and McGregor lambs with blue.*

*Some sheep would be set aside for market to raise much needed cash, and each clan would select a good meaty sheep for slaughter for their spring feast.*

*The round-up would start at first light on the appointed day and everyone who was fit and able took part.*

*This important day in the year was anticipated with huge excitement especially by the younger members of the families.*

*It was exhilarating to go out on the search, climbing up the craggy mountains with the sheepdogs.*

Rory McGlade, a red -headed strongly built 15- year-old, was allowed to work on his own for the first time this year with his adored dog Lexy. He was excited and proud to be entrusted with this responsibility and had worked all day to fulfil his obligations by finding and gathering in every single sheep in his allotted area.

The sun was going down fast now and Rory knew it was time to head home. As he strained his eyes and ears to check for any straggler, Lexy began to yap excitedly.

"Come on wee one, it's time to get on back. What's wrong wi' ye?"

He spoke calmly as he approached the dog whom he now saw seemed to be yapping at two rocks which leant against each other.

"What have ye found in there Lexy?"

Calming the dog down by speaking softly and stroking her head, he peered between the two rocks.

"Och, wee beauty, don't be afeared"

Gently Rory freed the young lamb from its imprisonment.

As he checked the animal over, he realised that it was not yet marked. He looked all around for the mother but to no avail. The light was fading fast now, and he knew he had to get back quickly.

Tucking the lamb under his arm and whistling Lexy to bring the small group of sheep together, he picked his way confidently down the mountain and back home.

*The lamb was put to suckle on a ewe whose own lamb had died and all seemed well.*

*Feast day arrived and the McGlades were noisily engaged in their celebrations when they were disturbed by a loud and insistent banging on the barn door. A young boy opened the door and Rory rose to greet his friend Angus McGregor who strode angrily into the middle of the gathering which had now become silent.*

*"Where is ma lamb? Its ewe is sufferin' terrible, she's engorged with milk and callin' for her bairn!"*

*Rory was shocked, "Angus, the lamb was trapped, it wasnae' marked..."*

*Before he could finish speaking Angus had stepped up and punched him hard in the face. Rory, knocked unconscious, fell to the floor.*

*Snatching up the lamb from the corner of the barn, Angus fled.*

*The McGlades gathered around Rory.*

*He was carried to his bed where his mother and father watched anxiously over him for two whole days until he woke from his coma.*

*As Rory grew stronger, he became aware that his brother and cousins were plotting a revenge attack against the McGregors. He felt desperately that this should not happen.*

*At last he managed to speak in a very weak voice,*

*"It wasna his fault... he was upset... his ewe was sae distressed... he's ma friend, we went to the school together... it was ma fault, I should ha' searched harder for the ewe..."*

*The eldest in the group, Duncan, who was a cousin of Rory's spoke;*

*"If he doesna want revenge we must respect that... but for the honour of Rory and all the clan we must seek an apology."*

*The next day three of the young McClouds made their way to the croft of Angus McGregor to demand that apology.*

*Unfortunately, the purpose of their visit was not known by the four McGregors they encountered on their way.*

*The McClouds were outnumbered and suffered a beating, but more than that, the pride of the clan was bruised.*

*Now instead of the understanding and forgiveness that Rory had sought there was even more mistrust and enmity between the clans. He felt completely responsible for this state of affairs which he knew could now lead to bloodshed. Rory tried desperately to reason with his family. He finally approached his grandfather Alistair, the chief of the clan.*

*Alistair however was a proud old warrior, stuck in his ways, and maybe a little feeble of mind. He relished the idea of the thrill of one last battle...*

Life seemed to go on as normal, but Rory knew that plans for attack were again being made.

He lay on the heather as his sheep grazed peacefully around him. His beloved Lexy sat beside him, her ears, eyes and nose alert to sheep that might stray, or an enemy that might presume to harm them.

"I know! A letter!" Rory sat bolt upright as the idea came to him.

That night whilst all his family slept, Rory composed his letter, the flame of the oil lamp flickering over his hesitant words.

**"Dear Angus**

**I am truly sorry that I brought your lamb home. I swear that I did not know that it was yours, I only wanted to save it, as any shepherd would.**

**Angus you were my friend once, why cannot we be friends again, like the smart wee laddies we once were?**

**All we need is a sign of apology from you that will satisfy my family.**

**Your sincere and faithful friend,**

**Rory McGlade"**

With a huge sigh and a hopeful heart Rory folded the letter and tucked it carefully into his leather money pouch.

After a troubled sleep Rory awoke at dawn.

*He and Lexy ran through the cool misty morning to Angus' croft.*

*Sitting on a heather-covered hillock with the croft in view and his arm around Lexy, Rory prayed in his heart that he could be friends with Angus once again.*

*Taking a deep breath, he stood up slowly. Now he took the letter from his pouch and the pair walked slowly on.*

*As they reached the door of the croft, Lexy yelped loudly and fell at his feet.*

*Rory knelt and took the dog tenderly in his arms. There was a deep gash above Lexy's eye, it was bleeding profusely. The distraught young man tried desperately to stop the blood flow. He tore off his plaid bandana, folded it into a pad and pressed it firmly onto the wound.*

*It was to no avail and when Rory realised that Lexy was going to die his anguished howl could be heard for miles around.*

*It awoke Angus. He was stricken when he saw his friend holding the dying animal - even more so when he noticed the McGregor arrow which had glanced off Lexy's skull.*

*With no hesitation Angus embraced his sobbing friend.*

*"Rory; the fight stops here... we'll ne'er be enemies again."*

*They buried the dog together; digging up the McGregor turf, gently laying the body, and reverently covering it.*

*The young friends went together to each of their leaders to explain that the conflict was over. The two clans united.*

*From then onwards the warriors of both clans fought side by side to champion the rights of the wronged and the weak.*

# ABOUT THE AUTHOR

Jane Nicholls grew up in Surrey. She attributes her ability to see all sides of a debate to being the middle child of five. The proud mother of ten children and grandmother to twenty, she now manages to devote more time to her other life-long passion which is writing. A nurturing and supportive tutor and students at a creative writing class helped Jane to produce numerous short stories and poems. Positive reactions to her work gave her the confidence to complete this, her first novel. She says that she has always been a writer and always will be.